Keela

Keela

JACLYN WEIST

Dragons & Fairy Tales Press

This is a work of fiction, and the views expressed herein are the sole responsibility of the author. Likewise, characters, places, and incidents are either the product of the author's imagination or are represented fictitiously, and any resemblance to actual persons, living or dead, or actual events or locales, is entirely coincidental.

Keela

Print ISBN: 978-1981861507

DEDICATION

For my husband. I'm so glad I found you.

Chapter One

Keela

Keela sat up and stretched on the sandy beach. She suddenly stopped. She wasn't supposed to be here. She was to meet her dearest Ronan outside her father's kingdom. Flashes of memory made Keela hold her head in agony.

They'd been caught. Father had never approved of their friendship, and had only grown angrier as the two had grown closer.

And now she was here. Keela glanced about, but didn't recognize the landscape. Where had her father sent her? At least her sealskin—no. She looked around, horrified. The skin that allowed her to become a Selkie was gone. She let out a sob as she searched frantically for it.

Voices echoed as they came closer to her hiding

place. Keela looked down at her legs in horror. They were only partially changed from her Selkie form. Whoever was coming could not see her like this. Trying to swim away at this point would be futile. Not without her skin. She grabbed at the sand, doing her best to hide her legs. If she could get them dry enough, maybe they would take their human form.

"I tell you, I saw something down here." The man's voice was gentle, calming.

Keela stopped scooping up the sand, mesmerized by the stranger.

"Conall, we came here for some peace and quiet, not for one of your hunts." A Leanan Sidhe. Keela knew it long before the woman came into view. The seductive power in her voice flowed through the air.

Keela had been foolish to stay here. She should have taken her chances by jumping back into the water. But it was too late now. She met eyes with the man. Conall? She ducked her head. She'd heard of a Conall once. He was a legend. And the fact that he was with the Leanan Sidhe sent Keela's mind reeling. It wasn't possible.

"See? I knew there was someone here." Conall held up his hands. "You have no need to worry. We're not here to hurt you. What's your name?"

Again, she felt the calming nature of his voice. She tried to resist it, but she couldn't help it. He was human— or he had been at one time. If legends were true, he'd lived over a hundred years before as a hunter until he fell in love with this Leanan Sidhe. He'd been transformed to a creature as powerful as the Leanan Sidhe.

"I am Keela." Her voice sounded strange outside of the water. She grabbed another handful of sand and patted it down.

The Leanan Sidhe frowned. "Why are you covering yourself in sand?"

"I . . ." Keela held her breath, trying to think of something. "I'm not clothed. Please leave me."

"Are you hurt?" The man took a step back, but didn't leave. "Do you need assistance?"

Keela shook her head. "No. Please go."

Conall and the woman glanced at each other and turned to leave. Keela breathed a sigh of relief that she was finally alone.

The footsteps stopped and the man came back. "You have no need to fear in this land. We will protect you. All you need to do is call my name and we will be there to help."

Keela stopped burying her legs and glanced up at him. The kindness in his eyes put her at ease, even after everything she'd heard about him. In desperation she asked, "Did you take it?"

"Take? Take what?"

"My . . ." She stared down at her legs, unable to speak it out loud. If she did, it would be true.

3

Understanding dawned on his face. "You're a Selkie?"

"Aye." Teardrops fell down her cheeks, something she wasn't used to either. "Did you take it?"

He shook his head. "I did not. But I will help you find the person responsible. If you need a place to stay, go up that path and find an inn. I'll look for you there."

"Thank you." Keela stared down at the sand, unable to speak. This man was a curious one, but the fact that he was willing to help gave her strength. The thought that he could be lying was there, but she knew through legends that he was true to his word.

As soon as they left, Keela stood and stretched her new legs. Until she found her skin, she would have to get used to them. The skin wasn't in the area. She would have felt it. Keela stared out at the sea. *I will find you, Ronan. That is my promise.*

The way out of the small cove was rough on Keela's hands and legs. She stumbled several times, scraping the skin. They would heal, but without her sealskin it would take much longer.

Strange carriages moved along the cobbled streets of the small village on the edge of the ocean. People moved along the sidewalks going about their business. Only a few looked over at Keela, and she preferred that. She looked down at herself. She needed to find something to cover herself and quickly. The coverings her father had given her did not keep out the cold and seemed to draw

4

attention. A small shop had a few racks of clothing out on the sidewalk. She waited for a group of people to walk by, then joined in. As they passed the rack, she grabbed a gown off a hanger and ran when shouts pierced the air. Her new legs didn't take her very far very fast, and someone grabbed onto her wrist.

The man holding her wrist glared at her. "You stole from the wrong person, lassie. It's off to jail for you."

"Please, no. I am cold." Keela handed the dress back to the man with her other hand.

"Then pay for it like everyone else does." He huffed and stomped back to his shop.

Keela held her wrist as she sought to find shelter. More people now stared at her, and she wondered if hiding in the cave below was the better idea. She cursed her father again for what he'd done to her.

A door down the road opened and loud music and laughter came from inside. Keela waited for a carriage to pass by before crossing the road. The sign above the door had a picture of a woman on it, along with writing. The reading lessons her father had given her did not pay off for the letters here were nothing like she'd seen before.

Another group of people came out of the door, and Keela was bathed in warmth for just a moment. She held the door open and paused for a moment before going inside. A woman sat on a stage singing about a poor sailor who lost the woman he loved.

Guests watched her sing while others sat at a bar

drinking something yellow in mugs. She slid along the wall toward the fireplace in the corner. Her hands and feet slowly thawed.

"Excuse me, lass, but I've been told to ask you to leave." A young woman stood behind her, smiling kindly.

"Is this not a place to get warmth and food?" Keela asked.

The girl nodded and glanced over her shoulder. "It's just that the state of your . . . dress is not good for the inn. I'm sorry."

Keela glanced down at her covering. "I tried to find something to wear, but the angry man wouldn't let me have it."

"Well, did you pay for it?"

"Pay?"

The young woman sighed. "Come with me. But do not speak. I could be fired for helping you. My name is Catriona, but most call me Triona. And yours?"

"Keela." She frowned. "Why would they not call you by your real name? Do they not like it?"

Triona laughed. "Triona is just a shorter version, and I like it better."

Strange customs. Keela followed Triona into a small bedroom in the back of the inn. Clothes hung on racks on one side of the room, and a bed and table sat on another side.

"Here. You're about my size. Change into this and

wash up at my sink. I will do something about shoes when I can. When you're ready, come and find me."

Keela stood in the center of the room holding the dress Triona gave her. Humans were strange creatures. This girl had told Keela to leave, only to provide clothing moments later. Keela would never understand them.

The dress was a little large on her shoulders, but it would do. The water in the basin was cold, but it would do. Keela washed her face and hands, enjoying the feel of water on her skin. This body was only temporary. She would have her sealskin back soon enough and she'd be able to go back into the ocean.

The main room of the inn had filled up more since Keela had left. Another lady now sang, and her words made Keela blush. She plugged her ears and turned to find Triona. The girl stood in the midst of several tables, talking to one of the men.

She looked up and smiled when she saw Keela. She finished talking, then beckoned Keela over to her. Triona handed a paper to a cook, then turned to Keela. "Are you hungry?"

Hunger? Keela hadn't thought of it since she awoke on the beach, but now her stomach growled. "Aye."

Triona took a bowl and took Keela's hand.

Keela jerked back. She would not be hurt again.

"It's okay. I was just going to show you where your table is. I'm sorry." Triona shook her head and moved

7

between the tables until she came to an empty one. "Eat quickly, then I'll put you to work."

"Work?"

Triona sighed. "You can't just eat the food and not pay for it. I'll get you a job here because you are in obvious need of some help."

"Thank you." Keela stared down at her bowl. It smelled good, but she didn't recognize anything in it. By that time, she didn't care. She needed food. Keela picked up her bowl tried to drink the liquid, but the broth was hot and scalded her mouth. She dropped the bowl, gasping and holding her mouth. She glared up at Triona.

"You don't eat the stew like that. Were you born yesterday?" Triona sighed and pulled a rag out of her belt, wiped up the spilled stew, then left the table.

Keela stared out the window at the ocean, mesmerized by the waves. She shouldn't be here right now. She should be out there with Ronan.

A *thunk* on the table made her jump. She looked down at the bowl of stew that Triona had set in front of her. Triona picked up a wooden instrument. "You use this spoon to get the soup, blow on it, and then take a bite."

The slightly patronizing tone that Triona used annoyed Keela, but she was too hungry to care. She did as Triona showed her and blew on the soup then took a small bite. The broth was like nothing she'd ever had before. She ate as quickly as the hot soup would allow her to, and soon she scraped the bottom of the bowl. She picked it up and licked the bottom, trying to get the last few drops.

"If you like it that much, I'll get you more. No need to make a scene." Triona took the bowl from her and went back to the kitchen.

Keela used her sleeve to wipe her face, then went back to staring out the window. The upbeat song the woman sang contrasted with the melancholy Keela felt inside. After another rousing song began, she'd had enough. She stood and walked to the front of the stage.

The singer stopped singing and stared at Keela. "Can I help you, lass?"

Keela took the instrument from her and strummed a few chords. She took the seat that the woman vacated and sat down. She began to sing, her melancholy pouring into the words. The inn disappeared as she went back to the kingdom she'd been banished from. To the man she loved. She sang of her lost love and the desire to return to him one day. The song had several verses, written by so many Selkies before her. It had been a warning to those who wanted to wander off to walk on land, but now it was a testament of everything Keela had lost.

When the last chords faded into the night, Keela opened her eyes. The inn was silent as the crowd sat overcome by the music. When Keela stood and handed off the instrument, cheers and screams for more erupted. Keela moved off the stage to get away from the angry customers.

"Wait. Don't go. They'd like to hear more." The woman on the stage held out her instrument.

Keela stopped, glancing between the stage and Triona who stood in the back with a look of shock on her face. Triona finally nodded and gestured toward the stage. Keela walked back to the stage and sat on the stool. This time she didn't use the instrument. Words rolled over her tongue that no one in the inn would understand. It was a lullaby that her mother had sung to her every night before she disappeared.

When Keela finished, there were cries for more, but she couldn't go on. She wanted to get back to the water, even if it was just to dip her feet into the sea. She bowed and left, ignoring Triona's pleas to stop.

She darted into the road and had to step back so she wouldn't be run over by a horse. The trip back to the cove was harder than it had been coming up, but she had to get back. Her feet bled as she ran across the sandy beach. The salt water stung the cuts on her feet, but she didn't care. Energy filled her, and the wounds healed themselves.

"Oh, Ronan, where are you?"

The ocean was silent. Even the crashing waves against the shore refused to speak to her. She was alone.

The sun slowly dipped into the horizon as she stood there. With a sigh, Keela turned and stepped out of the water. She needed to get back up to the village while there was light or she would have a hard time seeing where to place her feet.

The village streets were nearly empty when she finally got to the top of the cliff. Shops were closed but inns still blazed with lights and she could hear the sounds of laughter in the night air. She entered the same inn as she had that morning and found Triona waiting a table near the back. Keela weaved her way through the tables and set a hand on Triona's shoulder.

Triona jumped and turned, her eyes widening. She smiled at the family she'd been talking to. "One moment please."

She grabbed Keela's arm and yanked her toward the small bedroom. "You caused quite an uproar earlier today. Who taught you to sing like that?"

"It is the song of my people." Keela rubbed her arm.

"The song of your people?" Triona raised her eyebrows. "You are a strange one. I suppose you're back for more food?"

Keela nodded. Triona went to her wardrobe and pulled out an old pair of shoes and a long scarf.

"Sit." Triona pointed to the bed. When Keela sat, Triona took her foot to put on a shoe and gasped. "What did you do to your feet?"

11

Keela frowned. "The pathway has many sharp edges. I healed them when I went into the water, but it appears I was not as careful coming back as I thought I had been."

Triona shook her head and slid a shoe onto Keela's foot. "You should not go walking near the water without shoes. It's dangerous. Wear these and they'll be better protected." Once the shoes were on, Triona tied a scarf around Keela's face. "We can't let anyone recognize you or they'll want you to sing again. I'm not about to let that happen."

"Do you not like my singing?" Keela asked.

"It's beautiful. But as soon as you stopped, we had to send several of our customers away because they got into fights over who would try to court you." Triona stood. "Now, I will get you some food and then we'll see what Da will do about a room. Do not draw attention to yourself or you will be kicked out. Do you understand?"

Keela nodded and stayed behind Triona as they walked to an empty booth. Keela stared out the window trying to find her ocean, but it was too dark. She turned to watch the people instead. They were fascinating to watch. Each group talking about things that she'd never even heard of before. She stood to get closer to one group of people who were sure they'd seen a man rising out of the water, but Triona returned right then with a bowl of stew.

"There you go." Triona wiped her hands. "I have to wait tables, but I'll be back. Don't move."

Keela nodded and continued staring at the people who were talking. Ronan? Would Father have sent him so close to her? Her heart lifted at the thought, even though she knew it wasn't possible. She stared down at her stew and took a bite. It was just as wonderful as it had been earlier that day, but it was gone too soon. Maybe Triona's father would have more. She stood to go find him, but Triona stood in her way with another bowl.

"I told you to stay here." Triona set the stew down. "You don't move until the last person has left."

"Who are those men over there?" Keela pointed to the people who had been talking of the man in the water.

Triona glanced behind her. "Those are fisherman. Pay them no mind. They always bring tales of mystical creatures."

"And you don't believe them?"

"Not when I hear the same stories every day. They get wilder with every telling." Triona smirked. "Pay them no mind."

Keela nodded. They had people in her kingdom who would tell such tales as well. Still, the description of the man did match how Ronan looked when he was human. Broad shouldered, muscled, a face of beauty unmatched by any human man. Keela turned back to her stew and ate quickly. She wanted to talk to these men, but she would have to do it without Triona knowing.

But the men got up and left, promising to be back when they were done with work the next day. The small amount of hope that Keela had of finding her Ronan died as the door closed behind them. She had lost her chance.

"Come with me, but say nothing. I don't want you giving Da any reason to kick you out. I haven't had a friend my age for a long time, and I don't intend to lose you."

Keela nodded and stood to follow Triona. She took the two bowls Triona and brought and walked to the kitchen with them. Fatigue made her move slowly, but she knew she must do as Triona asked.

"Da, I'm going to take the key to the small bedroom at the end of the hall for Keela here. Is that all right?"

"Keela? Who is Keela?" The large man didn't look up from the meat he prepared in front of him.

"My friend, Da. The one I told you about." Triona pulled a branch of a plant off and handed it to her father.

He shoved it into the meat and set the pan inside the stove, then turned to Triona. "Now, where is this friend—" His eyes grew wide. "You. Get out."

"No, Da. She needs to stay. She has nowhere to go."

"That is not my concern. I don't allow anyone to cause trouble in my inn and I have to replace three chairs and a table because of her." His chest heaved as he stared down at his daughter.

Triona patted her father's arm. "Da, breathe. Keela

promised she wouldn't sing again. Please just let her sleep here for tonight. She can work off the cost of the room and the stew she's eaten."

"No. Send her to the inn next door. They have plenty of beds."

Keela watched the exchange in fascination. If she weren't so tired, she could have watched them for hours. Humans seemed to argue as much as she had with her father. Keela yawned and swayed on her feet. Being away from the water wore her down quickly, but after walking up and down the cliff twice, she could barely stay awake.

The sound of their voices faded as Keela's eyes finally closed. She felt strong arms scoop her up, and then darkness welcomed her.

Chapter Two

Ronan

Ronan pushed himself up to a sitting position and gasped. Blood ran down from a cut on his forehead from where Keela's father had struck him. He should have never gone to her that day. He should have listened to his mother.

The land he sat on was unfamiliar to him, but that meant nothing. He'd only been to the land near their home. He much preferred life underwater. The sun was still high in the sky, but the air was cold. It was no surprise that he no longer had his seal skin. Keela's father had been beyond reason. Fear struck him. Where was Keela? Was she a servant to a human? He needed to find her before that happened.

He stood and balanced before taking any steps. The

world spun for a moment, but then righted itself. Ronan stumbled over to the water and knelt in the water to wash the cut on his forehead. No need to scare the humans. He needed them to help him find his sweet Keela.

The nearest village was quite a walk from here, but he needed to find shelter soon. He couldn't regulate his human temperature as well as he could as a seal. He found a long pole and used it as a walking stick. The extra balance helped until he could get used to being on his feet.

A light drizzle began to fall, soaking Ronan. He picked up the pace and made it into the village by midday. Most of the inns were closed or full. A few eyed him suspiciously and told him to move on.

He moved off the main road and found a small rundown inn. It wasn't much to look at, but as long as it got him out of the rain, he would be fine. The room was busier than he would have thought, but then the rain had turned to a downpour in the last hour.

"May I help you, sir?" The innkeeper was a big man, but he only came up to Ronan's chin.

"I require food and a place to warm up." It wasn't a request, and the innkeeper knew it.

The man nodded and scurried into the kitchen. Ronan sat at the table closest to the fireplace to warm himself. He nodded to the innkeeper and ate the lamb, potatoes, and roll that was set in front of him. The innkeeper was there as soon as the plate was empty.

"Would you care for some more, sir?"

"No. I need to sleep. Do you have a room available?"

The man raised his eyebrows. "Do you have the coins to pay for the room?"

Ronan glared, but the man didn't back down. "Fine. I shall just sit here by the fire then."

"Very well. Just don't scare away my customers." The innkeeper waved to a man who entered and hurried off to talk to him.

Ronan turned his back to the front door and stared into the fire. He had to find some way to find Keela and then find both seal skins before someone else took them. It was quite a large task, but he was willing to do anything to be reunited with her again and to return back to the sea.

The rain hadn't let up by the time the dinner crowd had thinned. Ronan yawned and stretched. He would need to sleep if he was going to begin his journey the next day. He stood to leave and find another inn or at least an alleyway where he could keep dry for the night.

The innkeeper stepped in front of the door. "Leaving so soon?"

Ronan reached for the door handle. "Aye. Thank you for the meal. I'll find a way to repay you."

Rain puddled on the floor of the inn within seconds of opening the door. Ronan stepped forward to leave, but the innkeeper pulled him back in and shut the door. "All right, I'll let you sleep here for the night. I can't let you go outside in this rain. But you best be off at first light or I'll have to put you to work for tomorrow's room."

"Thank you, sir." Ronan bowed slightly. He shivered from the cold rain that had drenched him. "I'll leave first thing. I've already stayed in one place for too long."

The innkeeper stepped back, fear in his eyes. "Are you running from the law? If so, I must ask you to leave."

"No, it's nothing like that. I am looking for someone and every minute I don't find her means that she is in danger."

"Ah. Who is this lady? Perhaps I've seen her."

Ronan smiled. "She's beautiful. Hair long and flowing, her eyes are as blue as the sky. No matter what form she takes, she is unforgettable."

The man cocked his head to the side. "Form?"

Ronan cringed at his blunder. "Forgive my words. I am fatigued. I just meant that she is always beautiful."

"I'd love to meet this beauty someday. I hope you can find her. Come, I'll take you to your room. It's small as all our others are full."

"It will do just fine." Ronan climbed the stairs behind the innkeeper and waited for the man to unlock to the door. A bed sat in the corner, nearly taking up the whole room. He went straight for it and dropped onto the mattress. It was full of bumps, but he didn't care. After some sleep, he'd go back to the ocean to replenish his energy, then head along the coast. He couldn't imagine Keela leaving the coast too far behind.

The innkeeper shut the door behind him, leaving Ronan to stare up at the ceiling. Rain pounded against the windows, lulling him to sleep. In his mind, Keela smiled, promising to be with him forever. He vowed that he would make sure that happened. No matter what it took.

Ronan gasped for air as he stumbled into the ocean. The night in the inn had been good for rest, but after helping with the morning dishes, he was already running low on energy. He'd have to stay closer to the coast as he walked to find Keela.

It wouldn't stay this way. As he remained away from the water, his body would get used to the air and he'd be fine. Not that he wanted to stay here for long. He intended to return to the water as soon as he could. Energy flowed through him until he was ready to walk again. He put on the shoes the innkeeper had given him, then began his journey.

The rain had ended sometime during the night, cleansing the earth. The road was mostly deserted, but every now and then he'd step off to the side to allow farmers the chance to pass him with their flocks of sheep. Such strange creatures. Why someone would want to keep them as pets was beyond him.

It was around midday when Ronan came to another town. He pulled several coins out of his pocket. The innkeeper had told him how much they were worth, but it meant nothing to Ronan. He just knew that he was hungry, and he hoped there was enough in his hand to get something to eat.

Several street vendors tried to sell him their wares, but he kept going until he found a vendor with salted pork and fish. He bought a few pieces of each, then continued walking. Snatches of conversation went on around him. Talk of sales or family woes, but nothing of a strange girl in the village. If Keela had been here, she would have been the talk of the town. It was time to move to the next village.

As evening drew nearer, a horse-drawn carriage came thundering toward him. At first, he thought they were simply in a hurry, but as they came closer, he could hear the yells from whoever was in the carriage.

Ronan stood in the center of the road and put a hand out, hoping his powers would work as a human. He sent calming waves toward the horse, then braced himself. As the horse went by, Ronan grabbed onto the reigns and jumped onto the horse. He laughed to himself. His quick reflexes and strength hadn't left him, even if his ability to become a Selkie had.

The horse finally slowed to a stop, and Ronan climbed down. He moved to pet the horse before jumping back. This was no horse.

"What are you doing here, Kelpie?" Ronan demanded.

The Kelpie simply grunted and threw its head in agitation. Ronan held onto the reigns until the creature calmed down. If this was a Kelpie, then what was it pulling? He didn't let go as he moved toward the carriage.

"Please spare my life," The creature pleaded. An old hag appeared at the window of the carriage. "The hunter is near and I must get away before he finds me."

The Cailleach, the hag who supposedly controlled weather. Ronan frowned. "Why is he after you?"

"I destroyed his crops with my deluge of rain when he sent the hounds after me. I have been on the run ever since."

Ronan stared toward the village she'd just left. "And he's behind you?"

"Aye. Getting ever closer. Let me go, and I will grant you a wish."

"Will you tell me where my seal skin is? Or where Keela is?"

The Cailleach laughed. "I don't deal in love, dearie. As for your seal skin, the information is kept from me. Whoever has it is disguised. Let me go."

Ronan stepped back, but kept the woman's gaze.

"Very well. But know that I'm only detaining him long enough to see what he knows about my beloved before I let him go and tell him exactly which direction you went."

The Cailleach hissed, then snapped the reigns and sent the Kelpie flying down the road. He wondered how she'd managed to trap a Kelpie, but it was too late to ask. Besides, he had other things in mind.

There weren't many hunters that Ronan knew of, but those he'd heard of seemed to know the name and location of every creature in Ireland and possibly Scotland. If anyone knew where to find Keela, it would be him.

The trick was to find the man, but if he was good, Ronan wouldn't have to worry about it. The hunter would find him.

It was another half hour before Ronan reached the village. He searched for the nicest inn and went inside. The furnishings were nicer than the place he'd stayed at in the last village. He wouldn't stay here, though. The money he was given wouldn't cover a place like this. It was the hope that he would find this hunter.

"Can I help you, sir?" A young maid curtsied in front of him, blushing.

"I'm looking for a man."

The maid tipped her head to the side. "Could you be more specific? There are many men here."

Ronan glanced around the room. The man wasn't here. "No, he's not here. Thank you for your assistance."

He left without waiting for her response. Instead of staying on the main road, Ronan went through alleyways to find an inn that would look out over the ocean. If the hunter was as close as the hag had said, the man would be through here. He'd sense Ronan and come for him.

The inn he chose was not as nice as the one he'd just been inside, but it was close. He paid for a room, then sat at a window so he could see the ocean. The waves crashed against the coast. Keela's father must have been very angry for it to be this unsettled.

"State your business." A man stood next to Ronan's table. Power emanated from him in waves. Stronger than Ronan had ever felt. His green eyes searched Ronan's, almost daring him to look away.

"I'm searching for something. I have done no harm, nor do I plan to."

That didn't seem to appease the man. In fact, it only seemed to agitate him more. The man slid into the booth across from Ronan. "What is it you're searching for?"

Ronan chose his words carefully. This man could destroy a person with the snap of his fingers. "My seal skin. It was taken from me."

The man muttered to himself as he rubbed his chin. He leaned forward. "Is there unrest among the Selkies?"

"Not that I am aware of. Why do you ask?" Hope rose in his chest. This man knew something.

"You are the second Selkie I have met in the last few

25

days who has lost their seal skin. I haven't seen your kind for decades. Mermaids, Kelpies, but not Selkies. Now you're appearing again."

Ronan studied the man. "Decades? How old are you?"

The man sighed and leaned back in his chair. "You wouldn't believe me if I told you."

"Try me."

"I was born in the early 1700s as a human. I changed to this when I was in my thirties. You can figure it out from there."

Ronan smiled. "Next you're going to tell me you're the Gancanagh I've heard tales about. The man who managed to woo a Leanan Sidhe."

The man laughed and held out a hand. "In the flesh. Well, as much as I can be. And yes, Leana is my wife. She'll be here later tonight."

"So it's true, then. The tales of your adventures have reached the depths of the ocean. It is nice to meet you in person."

"It's nice for those who haven't caused harm, you mean. So tell me. Is the Selkie you're looking for a young woman? Blonde hair, piercing blue eyes?"

Ronan's breath caught in his throat. "You've seen her? Where? Is she all right?"

"She's fine. Or, she was when I left her two days ago. She'd just come from the ocean and was searching for her seal skin." His eyes met Ronan's. "Who did this to you?"

Memories from that day came back to Ronan. Meeting her in the garden. Being ambushed by father's guards. The so-called trial that ended up with both of them exiled. "Her father. He did not approve of our union."

Conall frowned. "He didn't approve so he sent you both into exile? He must be a harsh ruler."

"He wanted Keela to marry a prince from another realm, but she had already fallen in love with me." Ronan stared out at the ocean. "By separating us from our seal skin, he doomed us to becoming slaves of whoever finds it before us. Yes, he was harsh. But I never expected him to treat his daughter in such a manner."

"Was she next in line?"

"No. She is the seventh daughter. He married the others off to princes, and it was supposed to be her turn." Ronan met Conall's eyes. "I must know where she is."

Conall nodded. "I must continue to hunt the hag who terrorized this village, so I can't take you to her. Head north along the road and you'll find Keela about a day's walk from here. When I'm done with this job, I'll be back to help you two find the skins."

"Why would you help us?"

"Because that's what I do. I eliminate those who do harm, and I help those who need help. Plus, I have seen

27

how much you two care for each other. I want to make sure you're together again." He stood. "Find her."

Ronan flagged down a maid. "I'd planned to eat down here, but I am more tired than I thought. Could you bring some meat and potatoes up to my room?"

The maid curtsied and hurried toward the kitchen. Ronan didn't want to wait any longer to leave, but he knew it would be foolish to leave this late at night. He only hoped that Keela would still be there.

Chapter Three

Keela

Keela sat near the water, soaking in the sun's rays. It had rained almost constantly since she came to land, and the warmth felt good on her skin. The cove brought peace after the chaos of the inn. With all of the rain, people had been stuck inside, which meant that tempers were high.

The sun dipped closer to the horizon, so she stood and slipped her shoes on. She needed to get back or Triona would worry. It was nice to have a friend who wanted nothing from her. The path up to the village was now familiar to her and she could find each step even as the sky grew darker.

Keela skirted past the man's dress shop to avoid his glare. Surely he could forgive her. She'd given the clothing back. She pulled her hair up and stuffed it inside her hood, then made sure it covered most of her face. If guests saw her, they'd demand to have her sing for them.

She nodded at Triona and went straight to the kitchen. She would have loved to stay in the main room and listen to the music, but it was too dangerous. Instead, Keela hung her cloak on a hook and tied her hair back so she could help with washing the dishes. It wasn't her favorite thing to do, but it helped pay for her room.

"There you are. I was beginning to worry." Bran, the innkeeper set a bowl of stew and a large chunk of bread on the table. "I saved you some dinner. Hurry up with those dishes and then you can eat."

"Thank you, sir." Keela scrubbed at the plates in the sink. Her sensitive skin was red and raw by the time she finished each night, but it was better than attempting to cook. She'd burned several dishes before Bran finally pulled her off cooking duty.

When the dishes were finally done and her food was gone, Keela was ready to drop. She stretched and walked out of the kitchen to go up to her room. She realized too late that she'd forgotten to disguise herself.

"Sing for us, please," a man asked. His eyes were filled with desperation.

Keela shook her head and backed away. "I'm sorry. I must go to sleep. It's been a long day."

"Just one song?"

Others joined in, and soon Bran and Triona came

out to see what the problem was. Bran glared at Keela and put a hand on her shoulder. "She will not sing tonight. If you leave for your home now, she will perform tomorrow night."

Keela gasped. She was sure he'd throw her out long before he'd allow her to sing again. Her heart lifted. She'd missed singing.

There was a mad scramble for the door as people left for their homes. Those who were staying at the inn rushed up to their rooms.

"I should have done that earlier." Bran chuckled. "Don't think you're not in trouble. I warned you to keep your head covered, but you neglected to do so."

"Da, leave her be. She had a long day and forgot."

Bran frowned. "I realize that, but there are rules for a reason. These men won't stop wanting her music until the day they die. And for her sake, I hope that is many years from now. Upstairs. Get some sleep. You have a long day tomorrow."

Keela curtsied and ran up to her room. She opened the windows to allow in the scent of the ocean, then sat down at the desk. She hummed to herself as she brushed her hair, thinking of Ronan. She knew she should be looking for him, but she'd found a place here.

A knock came at the door, pulling her out of her thoughts. Keela stood and answered the door to find Bran standing there with his hands on his hips.

"What did I say about singing?"

"I wasn't. I promise." Fear bubbled.

Bran gestured to the window. "Look outside."

Keela ran to the window to find several men standing outside staring up at her room. The torchlight from the streets showed the hunger in their eyes. Bran stepped in front of her and shut the windows.

"I'm sorry. If you want to sing, I can't allow you to keep the window open." He wouldn't meet her eyes as he left the room, closing the door behind him.

"I wasn't singing," she said softly. How had they heard the humming? Was her magic so powerful? She climbed into bed and tried to sleep, but it evaded her. Noises came from below. She went to the window and saw that the crowd was still there. She listened for anyone coming to the door, then sang a lullaby her mother had sung to her as a child. Slowly, the crowd quieted and wandered off to their homes. That would only appease them until morning, but at least this way she could finally get some sleep.

The inn was unusually full the next day. Keela kept her head covered and moved quickly between cleaning tables and washing dishes. Anything to keep her occupied. There was still no sign of Ronan, and Keela knew it was time for her to leave this place. She would sing that night and then go to find him.

Except . . . the thought of leaving made her sick to her stomach. Something kept her here. She suddenly froze as she reached for a plate. Her seal skin. It had to be here somewhere. Otherwise, this village, these people would have no control over her.

Keela wasn't sure if she was relieved or horrified. This meant that she would be able to find it and go home, but if whoever had it knew what they held, she could be stuck as their slave.

"Hurry with those dishes, Keela. We have tables to clean off." Bran's voice was jarring in her ears.

She nodded and scrubbed the plate she'd been holding. Could Bran have it? Possibly. He seemed to know she wasn't what she pretended to be. But he was kind. He wouldn't keep her a slave. He'd threatened to kick her out every day if she didn't do what was required of her.

Triona wouldn't have taken it. But any of the men at the inn could have. It had been there on the beach. Keela set the last dish into the drying rack and grabbed the basket so she could clean off the tables.

The regular singer was onstage singing an old drinking song while Keela picked up all the dirty dishes. The woman was good, but she didn't hold the attention of the men as well as Keela did. It was probably better that way.

Keela watched for anyone suspicious, but no one

33

paid her any attention. So maybe no one actually had it yet. Perhaps she'd just missed it on the shore and it was still down there somewhere. Except that she'd walked the beach several times over the last couple of days.

Triona met Keela in the kitchen and took the basket out of her hands. "Da said he'd take care of the dishes. Come with me."

Keela barely kept up with her as Triona pulled her out of the inn and down the road to a dress shop. "What are we doing here?"

"Shopping. Da gave me some money to buy you a dress for tonight. I'm bigger than you, so the clothes you're wearing don't fit well enough to be up there singing."

"I have sung before. Why did he not care then?" Keela wandered through the store, touching the different fabrics. She stopped at a blue gown that flowed to the floor. It was different than anything else in the store. She didn't know what the cost was, but she was sure it was more than what the innkeeper could afford.

Triona pulled it off the rack and held it up to Keela. "This one. You need this one."

"But—" It was no use.

Triona had already left to find the shopkeeper. They talked for a moment before Triona pulled Keela toward a small room. "Try this on."

Keela stared down at the dress that Triona had

shoved into her hands. It was something royalty would wear. And while she wasn't royalty on land, she was in her own kingdom. She changed into the dress and studied herself in the mirror. It was as if the dress was made for her.

"Are you all right, Keela?" Triona's voice was outside the curtain. "Does the dress fit?"

"Aye." Keela pulled the curtain back and Triona gasped, her hands flying up to cover her mouth.

"It's beautiful." Triona walked around her, studying the dress. "This is perfect."

Keela smoothed the dress, loving how it felt in her hands. How the color reminded her of the sky. "I can't take this. I have not made enough."

Triona sighed and pulled out a satchel. "I told you that Da sent money with me."

Keela went back into the small room and changed into her other clothes, then met Triona by the shopkeeper. The old woman counted the money and put it in her purse, then went to back of the shop without a word.

"That was odd. Why didn't she ask you for more? This dress is clearly superior to most of the dresses in this shop."

"She doesn't know where it came from. Just showed up this morning." Triona left the shop and stopped at a vendor to get a meat pie for both of them. "Don't get this on the dress."

Her words unsettled Keela. Not about the meat pie. She already knew to wait until they were back at the inn. But who would have dropped off the dress? Who knew she was going to buy one today? Bran, of course. But why would he drop it off if he could just give it to Keela? She held back as they approached the inn. She wasn't sure she wanted to go in right then.

"Are you coming?" Triona stood with her hand on the door.

Keela glanced toward the ocean, but went inside. She wanted to tell Bran she was grateful for the dress, and skipping work wasn't the way to do it. Triona went to find Bran while Keela took the dress upstairs. She hung it up on a hook and stepped back. The dress was beautiful. And it was hers. No matter how it had come to the shop, it was hers.

Her heart was light as she went back downstairs to help in the kitchen. Bran stood at the stove and looked up when Keela walked in.

"There you are. Triona says you found the perfect dress."

"It's beautiful. Thank you for buying it for me." Keela took the pot from the fire place and poured the hot water into the sink so she could wash dishes. The thought crossed her mind again that it could have been Bran that gave it to her, but she brushed it away. When she showed up on stage wearing it that evening, she would know by his expression if he'd seen it before. If he seemed to know the dress, she could plan from there.

"Are you sure you don't want me to pull your hair up? It would look nice with this dress." Triona brushed through Keela's hair.

"I want it down. I don't get to wear it down often." The words came with a touch of bitterness that she wished she could take back. "I'm sorry. I understand why your father has me hide it. I should have said nothing."

Triona stepped back. "I understand. Sometimes we don't like how things are even when we know it's for our own protection."

Keela stood and smoothed out her dress. She would be singing soon, which meant she needed to get downstairs. "Thank you for helping with my hair."

Triona smiled. "You're welcome. I must go find Father. I'll see you down there."

Keela shivered as Triona left. They'd had the window open, and a cold breeze had picked up. She shut the window and stood there watching for Ronan. Where was he? She sighed and walked downstairs.

All eyes were on Keela as she walked over to the wall to wait for the other singer to end. Some still listened to the woman, but most stared hungrily at Keela. Maybe she should have insisted on not singing that night.

As the last note faded into silence, the other woman curtsied and fled the stage in tears. Keela felt a twinge of guilt. Birgit had worked here for many years according to Triona, and Keela had taken away all of her listeners.

Bran stood to the side of the crowd and nodded to Keela to go to the front. It was time. It wasn't that she was nervous. She knew what her singing could do. If she hadn't before, last night had shown her that she could have power over humans. It was the Selkie way. No, her hesitation was due to what could happen when she was done. These were good people. She didn't want to cause them harm.

She sang the first few words to a ballad that her father had written when her last sister had been married. And just like that, every eye was on her. Those who were eating stopped with their spoons halfway to their mouth. Triona stood in the back smiling. She wore earplugs so she wouldn't have the full effect of the song, and hers was the only expression in the inn that wasn't mesmerized.

When that song was over, the audience still sat in a trance. Keela glanced back at Triona. What was she supposed to do now? Triona waved to Keela to keep going.

The next song was a haunting melody. Tears ran down her cheeks as she sang, wishing that her beloved was there. She closed her eyes so she wouldn't have to see the tears on the faces of those listening. It was too hard to finish the song as it was. But then the door opened. Strange. Her powers should have been enough to mesmerize the whole village.

Thundering footsteps came toward her and before she could see who it was, Keela was picked up and spun around. When the man finally put her down, she pulled away, ready to fight her assailant.

Her breath caught. "Ronan."

"I have walked nonstop for three days trying to find you." He pulled her in for a kiss. His familiar scent was almost too much for Keela as she melted into his arms.

"How did you find me? I wanted to look for you, but I haven't been able to get away."

"Conall told me where you were." He kissed her again and scooped her up in his arms.

They could leave. Be alone. She had her Ronan back. He turned to take her away and faced the audience.

Keela's spell had already begun to wear off. The blank looks were turning to anger. "Put me down. Meet me in the back as soon as I'm done here."

"But—"

"Please." Keela placed her hand on his cheek, then began singing again. She moved to the lullaby she'd sung the night before. As she sang, she pushed the thoughts into their minds that they needed to go home. One by one, the audience stood and either left the inn or went up

39

to their rooms. When every person had left, she changed
the melody just slightly so they would forget most of this
had happened. They would hopefully remember that she
had sung that night, but not that Ronan had appeared, or
that she'd ended early.

Soon it was only Ronan and Triona left in the room.
Keela weaved through the tables and threw her arms
around Ronan's neck.

"I never thought I would see you again."

He brushed her hair out of her face. "My sweet
Keela. I would cross the world for you."

Triona cleared her throat and pulled her earplugs
from her ears. "This is Ronan?"

"Oh, yes." Keela smiled. "This is Ronan. And this is
my friend Triona. She has cared for me since I came into
the village."

Ronan took her hand in his and kissed it. "Thank
you for treating her well."

Triona blushed. "You are welcome. But I suggest
you two leave soon. As soon as everyone wakes, they'll
be looking for the man who stole Keela's heart."

Keela nodded. "We will require a room for Ronan.
But first I must speak with him in private."

Triona walked upstairs with them and opened the
door to the room next to Keela's, then went to her own
room.

Keela walked into Ronan's room with him. It was

40

furnished the same as hers, but the bed was on the opposite side. She made sure the windows and door were closed before she spoke.

Ronan sat at the small table. His eyes had dark circles under them, and he'd grown a beard over the last few days. "What is it that you wanted to speak with me about?"

"My seal skin. I think it's here." She whispered the words. Even though Triona was the only one in the inn awake, she worried someone would hear.

"Are you sure?" He clasped her hands in his. "That means we just need to find it and then we can look for mine before we head back to your kingdom."

The words should have made Keela happy, but the thought of returning to her father left an empty feeling inside. "You don't know where yours is?"

"No, but Conall has promised to help us." Ronan squeezed her hand. "But even if I don't find it, I will be fine. I have you back with me."

Keela's heart soared. "I didn't even know where to start looking. Every time I thought of leaving, something stopped me. I'm sorry I didn't go after you."

"It was better that you stayed in one place. It would have been impossible to find each other if we both searched."

"I feel as though I failed you nonetheless." She kissed his hands. "I have missed you."

Ronan's smile lit up his face. "And I have missed you. I say we wait no longer. Let's marry tonight. Then your father will not be able to pull us apart again."

Keela nodded. "Yes, although it might have to wait until tomorrow. I put everyone to sleep for the night."

He laughed. "Yes, I saw that. Some slept while they swept their steps. I see that your mother's talent was passed down to you."

"Someone had to gain the power. None of my sisters could do the same." Keela stood. "I must head to my room to sleep. Tomorrow we wed."

Ronan stood and pulled her into a hug. "Until tomorrow, then. I have waited this long, I can wait one more day."

She touched his face and walked into her room. But sleep wouldn't come. Excitement and guilt kept her awake. As dawn approached, she climbed out of bed and ran toward the cove. The tide was high, concealing much of the beach. She stepped into the waves and climbed up onto to a rock.

"Daddy. I hope you can hear me wherever you are. Ronan found me last night, Daddy. And I plan to marry him. Today. I hope that even after you were so angry, I can have your blessing."

Silence. Nothing but the waves crashing and seagulls overhead. Her tears mixed with the waves as she waited for a response. When nothing came, she climbed down from the rocks. Her new dress should have been soaked, but the water seemed to flow off of it.

"You look beautiful, daughter." A voice she'd known since the day she was born.

Keela whipped around. "Daddy? How? How are you here?"

He didn't say anything as he moved to the sand where she stood, then touched her cheek. "Seven of your tears fell into the water. It is an old tradition that when a maiden cries into the water, a Selkie will come to your aid. I heard your words, my flower. I have regretted exiling you since the moment I did so. Please forgive your father."

Keela reached up and hugged him tightly. "I forgive you."

"You have my blessing for this wedding. But please hold it in my kingdom so I can attend. That is all I ask."

"Don't you mean so that you and Mother can attend?" He was always forgetting her.

Father nodded. "Of course."

"Does she even know you're here?"

"No, she's too busy with one of her charity things. Please. Come home with me. We can surprise her."

"I cannot. We haven't found either seal skin." Keela stepped back to search his face. He should have known that already. "What have you done with them?"

Her father seemed troubled. "They should have

43

been easy to find. One is in the village above. The other was near where Ronan washed up on shore. It was the hope that some young man would find yours and you would fall in love with him. I even provided a dress for you to wear for your wedding." He gestured to the gown she wore. "I see you found that at least."

Keela stepped back again. Her father had not come to seek forgiveness. "Why would you want me to marry a human? You don't even like them."

"Anything is better than marrying below your station." But his face crumpled as he spoke. "Find your skin and come home. We will feast."

"Goodbye, Father. Tell Mother hello for me." Keela turned and ran toward the village.

Stones bit into her hands and feet as she climbed the hill to get away. She passed Triona and ran up to her room, ignoring the pleas to stop. Her breathing was heavy as she leaned against the door. She should never have talked to her father. She pulled on the dress to get it off. What once fit her so nicely now felt like it was suffocating her. Even as she was tearing at it, the fabric remained unharmed. She threw it across the room and dropped onto her bed. The long sleepless night and dealing with her dad left her exhausted and she fell into a fitful sleep.

Her dreams went between someone taking her seal skin and making her a slave, to her father crashing their wedding so he could drag Ronan off. She awoke suddenly and bolted upright. Something had awakened her. A knock at the door.

She climbed out of bed and went to answer the door. Triona stood in the hallway with a tray of food. Her eyes widened, and Keela looked down, realizing she hadn't put on anything over her shift. She slammed the door and slipped on Triona's old dress before answering the door again.

"Ronan has been beside himself all day. Are you ill?"

"No, but I slept very little last night." She took the tray from Triona and ate as quickly as she could, shoving the bread into her mouth. There was too much to do to be sitting in her room all day.

Triona curled her lip. "Please slow down before you choke."

"I cannot. I must go speak to Ronan." Keela slipped on her shoes and pulled her hair up.

"He's not here. He's tracking down a pastor." Triona glared. "You didn't tell me you were betrothed."

Keela frowned. "I must have at one point."

"No, you didn't. I would have remembered something like that." Triona stood and took the tray. "Come, let's talk to Da about the wedding feast. You already have a gown . . . what's wrong?"

Keela huffed. "I will not wear that dress ever again. My father made that for me, hoping that I would marry someone else."

Triona laughed. "Just because he made it for that purpose doesn't mean you shouldn't wear it. In fact, you should wear it just to spite him."

Keela stared down at the gown. "I shouldn't."

"You should." Triona went on about the feast and how she needed to make sure a goose was ordered for the occasion.

Ronan was still nowhere to be found when they got down to the main room, and Keela worried that he'd been taken again. She wouldn't have put it past Father to do so. She stopped short when she passed a table and turned around.

"Conall? What are you doing here? Ronan told me you had a job to do."

"He finished his job. We couldn't miss the wedding." Leana smiled and slid a small box across the table. "For you."

Keela hesitated before picking up the box. Inside was a small Claddagh ring. "It's beautiful. Thank you."

The door opened, letting in a cool ocean breeze. Ronan walked in holding a large box of produce. He smiled and dropped the box on a table, ignoring the angry protest from the patrons sitting there. He covered the space in two steps and swept Keela up in a hug.

"I thought you'd had second thoughts about the wedding."

"Never." She kissed him and pulled away to look into his eyes. "I went . . ." She realized she had an audience. "Come with me."

She waited until they were up in her room before explaining what had happened with her father that morning. By the time she was done, Ronan was pacing the floor, his jaw clenched.

"Did you find a pastor?" she asked, trying to change the subject.

He nodded and finally stopped pacing. "He will be here at sunset so we have time to get everything else in order."

Keela wrapped her arms around his neck. "Well, then I guess we had better get to work."

The inn was chaotic as people rushed about decorating for the wedding. Keela couldn't believe how quickly they'd stepped in to prepare a wedding for her when she'd only been there for a few short days. When she tried to say something to Triona, the girl simply laughed and said it's what they do for family.

Family. It was something that Keela should have had among her Selkie people, but she'd never felt it. If she were to be honest with herself, everything she needed was here in this inn. Except for her seal skin.

"What are you thinking about?" Ronan stood next to her holding a basket of flowers.

"It's nothing." Keela sighed. "I just wish I knew where to find the seal skin. Both of them."

Ronan leaned close. "That's why Conall is here. He will help us find both of them. I promise. Now cheer up

47

before I worry that you're not happy to be getting married."

Keela took a flower from the basket and put it behind Ronan's ear. "You will never have to worry about that. I am yours. Always and forever."

Chapter Four

Ronan

Ronan adjusted his suit coat. Weddings were much simpler in the Selkie culture. They didn't have to wear such uncomfortable clothing. But it was worth it. Music played in the other room indicating that the wedding would begin soon.

Bran indicated where Ronan was to stand. The pastor stood in the front of the room and nodded to Ronan, then signaled for the orchestra to play. Keela came toward him, breathtaking in the gown she wore. Her long hair flowed behind her with flowers woven throughout it. Her eyes danced as she stood in front of him.

The wedding was simple in the tradition of the Irish people. This was one reason he was glad they were on land. The Selkie tradition would have gone on for days.

As he leaned to kiss his beautiful bride, a loud thump sounded from the back of the inn.

"Step away from my property." A man stood there with a cane in one hand.

Keela gasped next to Ronan. "You."

"You know him?"

"I tried to borrow some clothes from his shop, but he tried to accuse me of stealing."

Ronan held in a sigh. Keela had never grasped the concept of borrowing. "What makes you say that she is your property? She is a free woman."

The man held up her seal skin. "This."

Keela let out a sob. "No."

"Where did you get that?" Ronan demanded.

"From a man. This morning. He brought it to me and promised me that I would have a wife if I just held onto this for him." He held it in the air. "This girl is a Selkie, friends. She has been fooling all of you."

"Leave her be. She has done you no harm." Bran pushed himself between the shopkeeper and Keela.

The man laughed and motioned to two men sitting at the back of the room. "She damaged a gown. I had to charge less for it."

"I did not. The dress was fine when you took it from me." Keela's face turned red as she stepped forward, but Bran held her back.

Ronan pulled Keela into his arms. "She's my wife. I need you to leave. Right now."

50

"Except I can't, you see. She's mine." He held up a contract along with the skin. "As long as I hold this. Take him, men."

Two officers stepped forward and grabbed Ronan's arms. He fought them off. "At least let me say goodbye to her."

They looked at each other, then at the shopkeeper before stepping back. The bulkier of the two folded his arms. "You have two minutes."

Ronan cupped Keela's face in his hands. "I love you. I'll be back, I promise."

Tears ran down Keela's cheeks. "Don't leave me."

"I found you once. I'll find you again." He kissed her, savoring the moment. As the men pulled him away, Ronan caught Conall's eye.

The man nodded, frowning. "Let this happen. I'll do what I can."

Rain poured down on them outside. Ronan was soaked through within seconds, but it didn't calm the fire in his heart. It was the same thing all over again. He was being taken away from his beloved by angry guards. But this time he was married to Keela. That brought a smile to his lips. It didn't matter what the man did. He wouldn't take that from them.

They stopped at an old building on the edge of town. The smaller man opened the door and they both shoved him inside.

"You can't keep me here. I had everything set before we were married. License, blessing from the priest. You have nothing to keep me locked up."

"Oh, you won't be locked up for long. The ship to Australia leaves in two days."

Australia? Dread filled him. He'd only heard of the country in passing. His kind stuck to Ireland and Scotland. He would be completely away from everything he knew. Away from Keela. That night was supposed to be wonderful, but instead he was alone. Again.

"Are you in there, Ronan?" Conall's voice came from the other side of the door.

Ronan jerked out of sleep and looked around, trying to remember where he was. He groaned and stood. "Conall?"

"Oh, good. I'd hoped to talk to you before they took you away."

Ronan went to the window. "They said I leave in two days. Which I guess would be tomorrow now."

"Aye. And you must get on that ship."

Ronan jerked back. "What do you mean?"

"From what I found out, your seal skin is going to be on that ship with other furs that they'll be trading down there."

Ronan's jaw dropped. "Where did you hear this?"

"Let's just say someone wants you as far away from his daughter as possible. These ships usually carry nothing but prisoners so that they can carry more people. But these furs were requested by the people down there because it expected to be a harsh winter."

"And you're sure it's in there?" But Ronan could sense that it was true. Conall had no reason to lie to him. He was known to be a man of his word.

"Aye. I have a feeling they know it's yours and that you'd make a perfect slave with your size. I tried to get my hands on it, but it was heavily guarded. I'm sorry." Conall leaned closer to the window. "Keep an eye out. Look for any possible chance to escape. If you make it all the way to Australia, you will lose your chance to be with your wife."

Ronan placed his hand on the window. "I don't know what I've done to deserve your assistance, but I want to thank you. Take care of my wife. I'll be back as soon as I can."

"I know you will. I'll make sure she gets her skin back as soon as possible." Conall went quiet. "There are people coming. Good luck."

Ronan slid down the wall and closed his eyes to get more sleep. There was nothing he could do from in here, so he had to trust this strange man.

The shipyards were loud and chaotic, which did nothing for Ronan's headache. He'd barely slept, and they'd only fed him twice in the two days he was stuck in the jail. Other prisoners seemed worse off than Ronan with their arms and ankles shackled.

Ronan was forced into a line as they made their way onto the ship. The two guards who had captured Ronan that night were gone, replaced by others who were less savory. While others stared at the ground or heckled the guards, Ronan kept his eyes closed, trying to sense his seal skin. It was here somewhere. He could feel it.

It was his turn to climb onto the ship. The charges against him were ridiculous. The one dress that Keela had taken had suddenly turned into ten, and Ronan had supposedly attacked the man. Ronan held his head high, knowing he hadn't done any of what they'd said. It was a miracle that Keela wasn't with him on the ship from the accusations.

He received his rations and followed the line of prisoners onto the ship. He searched for any sign of the crates of furs, but they must have been stored already.

"Hey, you. Eyes straight forward. No getting any ideas." The guard shoved him into the man in front of him and laughed.

The man turned and glared, but when he saw Ronan's size, he quickly turned and said nothing. Maybe Ronan could survive this after all. He was a gentle man by nature. Too soft as his dad liked to tell him. But if he had to seem imposing to get through this, he would.

He was shoved into a cell with several other inmates. There was very little space to sit, so Ronan sat on the ground and closed his eyes. Might as well get comfortable. He would be stuck here for months. Or at least until he could find his seal skin.

It seemed like hours before the ship finally started moving. The waters were choppy in the shallow waters, and several of the inmates were sick within the first hour. Ronan smiled. These waves were like coming home to him. And the farther they got out to sea, the more energy he felt. Yes, he could handle this. He just had to keep looking forward to the day he would be reunited with Keela.

Chapter Five

Keela

Keela looked up from scrubbing the floor and glared at Maurice, the shopkeeper. He'd had her working nonstop since he'd ruined her wedding days before. While he stood there picking his teeth, she was forced to scrub floors or wash the walls. The constant rain made it nearly impossible to keep up with the muddy footprints brought in by customers, but he wouldn't let up.

Triona had tried to come over the first two days, but he had been so horrible to her, she simply waved when she went by. Something was going to change. It had to or Keela would go mad.

"That spot is good enough. I want my windows washed." He gestured toward the front windows that she'd washed the day before.

"But they're still clean."

He glared. "Do you dare test me?"

She was a princess to a sea king, the wife to a wonderful, hardworking man. She shouldn't have to be in this position. She straightened and stood. "You will not speak to me in that way."

"Oh, I will, lass. I can speak however I want. Judge said so." He laughed and threw a rag at her. "Now get out there and work."

Keela grumbled and stomped out to the front window. A group of high society women walked by and stared at her, then burst into laughter. She gripped the rag in her hand, imagining how satisfying it would be if she could just throw it at their head.

Maurice came out of the shop and set one of his newest gowns out on the rack. The women immediately turned around and came back to look at his merchandise. Keela rolled her eyes and went back to washing the window in front of her. Never mind that they were now dirtier than they'd been before she started.

As soon as he had the women roped in, Keela slid into the alleyway and took off sprinting. She wouldn't be able to go far. Not now that she was held a slave. But she had some words to say to the man who had caused this. Maurice had assumed that relieving Keela of her shoes would keep her from getting away, but he clearly didn't know her.

It wasn't hard to produce the tears that it would take to summon her father. She simply had to think of the man who was a prisoner on a ship headed for Australia. As soon as the tears flowed, she wiped her cheeks and washed them in the waves.

"Father. I must speak with you. Now." She never would have dared speak to him that way before. But he'd crossed a line. Many lines, actually.

Her father appeared. "So, I'm father now? What happened to Daddy?"

Keela clenched her fists and stepped farther into the water. "Maurice happened. Father, how could you? I was your youngest child. I was taught since I was a child how special I was, how lucky you were to have seven daughters. And now you throw me away as if I were rubbish."

"You did this yourself, child. I warned you what would happen if you didn't obey, but you did it anyway. Your marriage to Ronan sealed your fate."

"So, you would sell me to the man who despises me most?"

He shrugged his shoulders. "Whatever it took to help you learn that I meant what I said. You know how to get out of it."

Keela's jaw dropped. "You would dare to blackmail me into coming home?"

"Not blackmail. Consider it a nudge. We need you

home, daughter. The kingdom is revolting without you there."

"Why? I have no power over them."

He sighed. "I would have thought the same thing, but it is not the case. Your sisters have all left the kingdom with their mates, leaving me to rule alone. They seem to think that I have lost my touch. I need you there to help get them under control."

Keela couldn't believe she was hearing this. The main reason she'd met Ronan in the first place was because she was escaping the palace to find someone who would care. Every day she'd been told that she would never rule, that it wasn't important for her to learn the politics behind the throne because it had no effect on her.

"They're right, Father. You have lost your touch. You do nothing to care for the poor. The sick have no medicine because you are set on making your castle more beautiful. Even the rich feel as they're uncared for. Now, I must get back to the prison that you set for me. I don't need your help. I will find a way out of this just as I have done so many times before."

Keela spun on her heel and headed back to the shop. She would pay for leaving if Maurice found that she'd left.

"I can stop him, you know. Just say the word and I can have you back here with me," her father called from behind her.

Those words just made her walk faster. If he thought she was helpless, he was going to be proven wrong several times over. Keela climbed up the hill and walked through the alley back to the shop. Her rag still sat where she'd dropped it. Voices came from the front. She peeked around the corner to see the women leaving the shop with packages in their arms. She sighed in relief. He had been too busy to know that she'd left.

Maurice came around the corner. "There you are. The windows can wait. I need you to meet my supplier outside of town. But hurry, I have orders I need to fill."

"You want me to go?" she asked in surprise. He hadn't let her out of his sight except to sleep since the morning after her wedding.

"I can't leave you here to watch my shop, now can I? You'd make off with all of my merchandise."

Keela opened her mouth to argue, but finally nodded. "Yes, sir. I'll be back by sundown."

"Not so fast, lass. You're not going alone. I don't trust you there either." He snapped his fingers, and a man came from somewhere down the street. "He'll tag along to make sure that you don't try any funny stuff."

Conall shook his head slightly when she opened her mouth to speak. He took her by the shoulder. "I'll make sure she does your bidding, sir."

"You'd better for the money I spent to have you in my service," Maurice said. "Go."

Conall guided her away and didn't let go of her shoulder until they were out of sight of the shop. Leana joined them shortly after and took Conall's hand.

"Please just let me drain him. It would take seconds." Leana glared over her shoulder.

"Not yet, love. We need him for a little longer." Conall smiled at Keela's look of horror. "Leana forgets her place when she's hungry. The man will get what is coming to him in the end, but for now he must believe he's in control."

"He's not?" Keela asked.

Conall laughed. "He believes he is, yes. But he's simply a pawn to get your seal skin back. He's also the reason your husband is within arm's reach of his."

Keela stopped. "So, it wasn't my father . . .?"

"No. Well, at first it was. Your father did give him the seal skin, but Maurice had no idea what it was. He'd planned to sell it in his shop. When I found him with it, I simply let it slip out what it was. From there, we were able to let the rest unfold."

Leana patted Conall on the arm. "My husband is wise beyond his years."

"Except for the fact that he didn't just snatch the seal skin out of Maurice's hands when he had the chance." Keela's anger flared. "I could have been freed from all of this and Ronan would be by my side."

Leana's hair flared red. "Do not speak to us in anger.

If Conall had stepped in and taken the skin, you would have had your freedom, but Ronan's would have been lost forever. It had to happen this way."

Keela felt as though she'd been slapped in the face. Leana was right. What good would it have done for to have her freedom when Ronan would have been cursed to live on land forever? She stayed silent the rest of the way out of the village.

A man stood with a wagon blocking the road into the village. He stood up straight as they got closer. His smile clearly said he was ready to sell them the entire wagon for the right price.

"Good morning, my fine people. I am in town just for the day with materials that will suit you. Would you care to see?"

"Not, this time, sir. We're here for Maurice's order only." Conall stepped forward to show that he was clearly in charge.

It annoyed Keela that Conall would take charge, but with a warning look from Leana, she stayed silent. The man's eyes narrowed when he realized he wasn't going to get what he wanted out of the three of them.

"I don't know what you're speaking of. I know no Maurice." His hand went to the knife in his belt.

Conall laughed. "Oh, I believe you do. I also know that you aren't all that you seem. Now, if you want to cause trouble, my wife and I can take care of you in a hurry."

"How dare you threaten me?" The man bristled.

Leana smiled and stepped around her husband. "Ooh, I didn't think I'd see you again so soon. You don't learn your lesson well, do you, Kelpie?"

Before either of them could react, the Kelpie struck out at them, grabbing them by their throats. Conall reached for his knife while Leana's hair burst into flame. The Kelpie yelped in pain, but kept its grasp on her.

"Sing," Conall gasped out.

Keela began singing the song she'd used to get the villagers to leave the inn. At first, it seemed the Kelpie was unaffected, but as the song went on, Keela added more feeling and power into the words. The Kelpie stumbled and blinked, giving Conall the chance to swipe at the arm holding him.

"Keeping singing," Conall shouted.

Keela jumped, and began singing again. Conall shoved the knife into the Kelpie, then reached for the bag he carried over his shoulder. He pulled out a bridle and dove forward to slide it onto the Kelpie's head.

Leana dropped to the ground, gasping for air. Keela didn't stop singing until Conall set a hand on her shoulder. She collapsed next to Leana from exhaustion. The energy it had taken to keep up the song had drained her. She needed to head back to the ocean as soon as possible.

"See, love? I told you this would come in handy."

Conall pulled the bridle off the dead Kelpie and put it back in his bag. "Shall we return to the village?"

Keela could barely move, let alone try to walk. "How do we get the supplies back to Maurice? He will be angry if we don't get them."

Conall patted the horse that was hooked to the trailer. "He'll take it for us. You two climb in back."

Leana stood and climbed up into the wagon, then Conall helped Keela in. The ride back was bumpy and uncomfortable since there was so many supplies inside. Several of the other shopkeepers followed close behind the wagon asking Conall questions about the contents of the trailer.

He stopped in front of the dress shop and waited for the women to climb down before turning to Maurice. "Your merchant was disposed of somewhere along the way, but we were able to save the rest of the wares from the thief. Take what you need, then we'll share the rest with the others who need it."

Maurice rubbed his hands together and snatched up as much of the fabric as he could in his arms. "Grab the rest of it, lass."

Keela curtsied and took what fabric she could carry and followed him. She stopped and looked over her shoulder. "Thank you."

Conall nodded and smiled. "You're most welcome."

The shop was dark after the sunlight. Maurice was

in the back of the shop sorting through the items. "I need more buttons and some ribbon. Go and see if he has anymore before the other vultures take it all."

Keela swayed with exhaustion as she walked back through the shop. She had to hold onto the wagon to stay upright. "Are there anymore buttons or ribbon?"

Leana grabbed a handful and dropped them into Keela's arms. "Are you well? You are pale."

"I need the ocean." Keela turned to leave, but Leana stopped her and took the items from her.

"Go. I'll take care of him." Leana's smile sent a chill down Keela's spine, but that wouldn't stop her from going to the water. Conall would watch Leana. She hoped.

The relief from the water was almost immediate. Keela didn't want to stay long for fear that her father would appear again, but she wanted to make sure that she was fully rejuvenated before she went back to face Maurice.

Keela had to admit to herself that the fight with the Kelpie had been quite exciting. She'd lived in a palace in her kingdom, and while she'd go off to visit the poor parts of the city, she hadn't had to deal with any fighting. That had been left to the soldiers. But now . . . she didn't have the powers of Leana or the strength of Conall, but she could sing. Perhaps they would let her help them fight while she awaited Ronan's return.

But first she would need to free herself from Maurice's grasp. Keela made her way back to the shop and found Leana flirting with Maurice. Conall stood a few feet away watching the two with an amused expression.

"You don't mind that she is speaking with him like that?" Keela asked.

"Better than having her suck his soul." He laughed and hooked his arm around Leana's waist. "I must get Leana home. I do apologize for the loss of your best supplier. Perhaps they'll send a new one through next month."

Maurice appeared dazed as they walked away, making Keela think that Leana had done a little more soul sucking than her husband realized.

"I am feeling unwell. May I leave?"

He simply nodded and turned to go back into the dress shop. Yes, Leana had most definitely done something. Keela hurried into the inn before he could change his mind. She didn't have her hair covered, but after the wedding had happened, most seemed to leave her alone. Having her seal skin might have also had something to do with it.

Triona waved at her and served a group of customers before coming over to where Keela stood. "You're back early. I wasn't expecting to see you until nightfall."

"Maurice took ill and allowed me to leave for the night." Keela yawned. "Would you like some help?"

"Everyone has been served, so I have things under control. You could help with the dishes later if you'd like."

Keela nodded and went into the kitchen to find some food. Bran handed her bowl of stew and a thick slice of bread.

"I wasn't expecting to see you until later. I'd planned to set this aside until you got back."

"He let me off early today." She took the bowl back into the main room and sat at a table. The stew and bread were exactly what she needed to build her energy. She took a bite and a burst of flavor she hadn't expected welcomed her. Bran had added shellfish into her stew. She hadn't tasted such perfection since she had arrived on land. She had to force herself to eat it slowly so she could savor the flavor. While she'd grown accustomed to the lamb stew, she preferred this.

As soon as she was done, she grabbed her bowl and took it into the kitchen, then threw her arms around Bran. "Thank you for the wonderful food."

"I thought you might like that." Bran chuckled. "As soon as I found out you were a Selkie, I sent out an order for the freshest seafood I could get my hands on."

"It was perfect." Keela peeked into the pot on the stove, earning another chuckle from Bran.

He took her bowl and filled it with more stew. "This is your last for the evening. We'll save the rest for tomorrow."

Keela stood in the corner of the kitchen and scooped food into her mouth. By the time she was done, her stomach was happy, and she could barely keep her eyes open. But she'd promised Triona that she would help with the dishes.

She added hot water to the sink and washed while Triona cleared the tables. It was past dark by the time they were done. Keela waited for Bran to leave the room, then told Triona what had happened earlier that day.

Triona's eyes were wide. "Your life is much more exciting than mine."

"Aye, but right now I would prefer your quiet life." Keela stretched. "I must sleep. Maurice will want me there early. If he doesn't drag me out of bed before I wake."

"That horrible man. He treats you so poorly. I wish we could free you from his grasp."

Keela sighed. "The only way to do that is to get my seal skin back. But I haven't been able to find it in his inventory. He has hidden it well."

"We will find it. Then you can become a Selkie and go find Ronan."

"I wish it were that easy. We don't leave these seas. It's too dangerous for our kind. Sea monsters live out there, keeping us from leaving Ireland and Scotland."

Triona frowned. "Will they do harm to the boat that Ronan is on?"

"Probably not. They are used to human ships." But then, would they sense Ronan on the ship? Possibly, but she hoped he would be safe. "Good night, Triona."

"Good night."

Keela took the stairs to her room and went straight to the window. She knew she couldn't see the ship from here, but it didn't stop her from looking to the south. Ronan was out there somewhere. She rubbed the ring on her finger, promising that he would always be true. She just hoped that they would see each other again soon.

Chapter Six

Ronan

Ronan drew another line on the wall of the ship. Another day done, and he was still stuck in a cell with the other inmates. If the shipment of furs was on here, he would never know. They were able to get up for meals and to walk around for a bit, but he hadn't seen the sun for weeks.

"Single line. Let's go." A guard stood at the door, ready to take them up to breakfast.

Ronan got into line with the rest of the prisoners, then waited to walk up. Everyone around him stayed a good arm's length away from him. Two scuffles and a few broken ribs, and they tended to respect a man. But it bothered him. He wasn't this person. This criminal. He'd had it rough growing up, but to have people want to fight him? That never happened.

Breakfast was the same as always. Gruel, bread, and today they also had a little fruit. To avoid scurvy, they said. Whatever that was. Ronan ate in silence at the end of the table. His heart ached constantly for his home. Not Ireland. The only thing there for him was his Keela. But the ocean. He hadn't touched seawater for weeks and he could feel himself dying slowly. The stale water at the bottom of the ship barely counted. All it got him was some time in solitary for breaking away from the group.

He was thankful when it was time to go back down to the cell. His bed was near one of the openings—the reason for one of the scuffles—and he could at least pretend that there was sunlight out there. As they passed a room, Ronan's ears caught a loud argument that had broken out. Something about land ahead, that sent a chill through Ronan. He stepped out of line and ducked down so his height wouldn't give him away.

Ronan peeked around the corner to find the captain and first chief at each other's throats arguing.

"I'm telling you, we're going too fast. We're going to hit land and kill everyone on here."

"And I'm telling you that we're fine. I've sailed this route countless times. Now get out of my office." The captain stared the other man down, but the first chief wouldn't budge.

"If you'd just go up and look instead of staying down here with your alcohol, you'd see what I'm talking about."

The captain put his hand on his hip, his face turning red. "I will have your job for such insubordination. Out of my office. Now."

The first chief stormed out of the office, stringed with obscenities. Ronan stood and stepped back in line with the rest of the prisoners. He didn't like where the conversation was going. If the first chief was right, there were over two hundred prisoners, and all of the crew that would pay for the captain's mistake.

The cells were locked down as soon as the last prisoner was accounted for. Ronan sat on his bed and whittled at the wood he'd been given like he did every day. They'd supposedly be able to sell them when they got to Australia. He didn't care what they did with the items. He just needed a way to pass the time.

"What do you know of the captain?" Ronan asked. The cell went silent as he suspected it would. He never spoke.

"Why do you ask?" one of the prisoners— Declan?—asked. He was technically the leader of the group, even though he still cowered when Ronan came near.

Ronan stayed silent for a moment, debating how much to let on. "Just wondered. Is he a good man? Smart?"

Declan leaned forward. "We have been sailing for three months, and now you ask about the captain? What are you up to, Ronan?"

"Nothing. I just heard something on my way back here that has me unsettled. I just wondered if there was a reason to worry."

Muttering broke out among the prisoners. Ronan locked eyes with Declan until the smaller man broke contact. He knew that Ronan would best him if they fought.

"Keep your worry to yourself until you have reason." Declan glared at him before turning to one of the other prisoners.

Ronan went back to whittling. Clearly he wouldn't get anywhere with the other prisoners. He would have to figure out how to break away from the group and investigate on his own. That would allow him to look for the furs as well.

Lunch was closely supervised, so it was nearly impossible to do anything without them knowing something was up. Ronan took his time eating, hoping for an opening where he could separate from the rest of his group.

A small man sat across from Ronan at the table. "I'd stay clear of the captain, if I were you."

"Why is that?" Ronan pushed his plate away and leaned on the table.

The man cleared his throat and waited for the guard to pass by. "Rumors. He can be reckless as a captain, but he also loves his alcohol. It's better to keep your head down and wait until we're off the ship."

Ronan nodded. "Thank you."

The man stood and went to line up to head back to the cells. Ronan finished his food and lined up so he could have a little more time to listen for anymore news. Guards stood near him as they walked back through the ship. So much for that.

It was two days later before Ronan finally had his chance. They were on their way back to their cells from having dinner when the group was held up.

"You there." A doctor stood in the hallway of the ship. He pointed at Ronan, and the two guards next to him grabbed Ronan's arms. "I haven't done your checkup yet. It's time."

Ronan had normally fought the checkups before this. No need for the doctor to figure that he wasn't a typical human. But this time he allowed the guards to pull him toward the doctor. The man had his own room near the families of the crew. He was an older man with a stooped back, but his eyes were sharp.

Ronan sat patiently while the doctor checked his ears, eyes, and throat. When it was time to check his heartbeat, Ronan kept moving just enough that the pulse was off.

"Please stay still. There is something off . . ."

Ronan climbed off the table. "Something is wrong because I've been sitting in one place for the last few months. I'm fine."

The doctor frowned. "Things are not as they seem, are they?"

"That would be the case, yes. As far as you're concerned, everything is normal. That's what your records will say."

The man nodded and waved him out of the room. "Watch yourself. There are some who would love the sport of tracking you down once you get there."

Ronan turned back. "I don't plan to be there."

The halls were clear as he walked back to the cell. The guards should have been there, but his physical had ended faster than most. He took advantage of the empty hallways and ran down the stairs, past another group of prisoners, and finally got to where they stored the supplies they'd be trading.

The crates were nailed shut, but that didn't keep Ronan out. A simple tug was all it took to open them. Spices, alcohol of all sorts, fabrics. But not furs. Shouts came from above. They'd noticed he was gone. He put the lids back onto the crates and headed for the stairs on the other side of the ship. Several more crates sat there. He suddenly stopped. There as something different about these. He felt . . . Footsteps clattered on the steps, so he had to run again. He'd have to come back later. He made it up to his cell before the guards finally caught up. He leaned against the door and calmed his breathing. "What took you so long?"

"Where were you?" a guard demanded.

"I don't know what you mean. I was with Dr. Donaghue and when no was outside waiting for me, I decided to come back here." Ronan stepped back so the guard could let him in. His heart was a little lighter as he climbed onto to his bed. He knew where his seal skin was. Now it was just a matter of getting ahold of it so he could escape. He'd waited months. He could wait just a little longer.

That night the atmosphere in the ship changed. Ronan wasn't the only one who felt it by the looks on the other prisoner's faces. Shouts sounded here and there as sailors rushed back and forth on the deck. Land was shouted a few times, but they were quickly quieted by more shouting.

Ronan reached out and grabbed a sailor's shoulder as the man passed. "What is happening?"

"Land. We're headed straight for it." The sailor yanked his shirt out of Ronan's hand and ran down the hall.

So he'd heard right. He cursed and turned to Declan. "Did you hear that?"

"Aye, and you can guarantee that we'll be the last to be saved if this ship sinks." Declan ran his mug across the bars, back and forth to get the guards' attention. "Let us out."

Others joined in. Ronan stared up at the hole that led to the top. He grabbed the nearest bed and shook it until the bolts came loose. He pulled it over under the hole and climbed up. He could reach about half way to the top. He needed another bed. With the help of a few other prisoners, he piled them on top of each other and climbed up.

He leaned over the side. "I'll come back when I have news."

Declan nodded and ordered the prisoners to put the beds back. No need to get them in trouble if a guard went through. Ronan broke into one of the guest cabins and grabbed the largest clothing he could find. The shirt was tight across his chest, but it would do. He grabbed the beard trimming scissors and chopped his hair off, then used the razor to shave his beard.

As soon as he was presentable, Ronan slipped out onto the deck. People moved about the ship as though everything was okay. Perhaps the sailor was wrong. Ronan ran to the bow of the ship and stared out at the ocean.

More yelling came from the captain's quarters. Ronan crept over to stand next to the door. He peeked inside to see two men standing face to face. It was the captain and first chief again. The chief stepped forward until he was just inches from the first chief.

"You will not undermine my authority. You are

causing undue panic among my crew, and I do not appreciate it."

"It is you who are in the wrong. There is land ahead and if you do not turn now, it will be too late. You must listen."

Ronan put his hand on the door knob to defend the first chief, but decided against it. He was a simple thief according to his record. They wouldn't listen. But the doctor would. He watched for guards as he ran for the doctor's room. He knocked on the door.

Dr. Donaghue opened the door. "Ronan. Shouldn't you be in your cell?"

"Yes, but you must speak to the captain. There is land ahead. He has been warned several times, but he isn't listening."

"You overestimate my authority here. They would no more listen to me than they would you." Dr. Donaghue chuckled. "Come in before you're discovered."

Ronan walked into the small room and sat on one of the chairs, then jumped back up again, too agitated. "If you can't speak to him, who can? If we continue on this course, hundreds will die."

"You must prepare the people to escape if needed. There are a few rescue boats, but not many. Save as many as you can."

Ronan stared at him. "That's it?"

"Unless you can do better than a shave and a haircut, then yes, that's all you can do." Dr. Donaghue stood. "Now go. I'll try to speak with the captain."

"Thank you." Ronan stood at the stairs. He was free. He could go get the seal skin right then and no one would know.

The ship creaked, knocking Ronan out of his thoughts. He couldn't leave now. It would be time for dinner soon so he had to move fast.

"Hey, Declan." Ronan stopped by his cell. "Spread the word. Land is just ahead of us and the captain isn't listening."

Declan's eyes widened. He nodded and spoke quietly to those around them. Ronan moved on to the next cell and said the same thing to them. Once every cell had been notified, he ran to the next deck and told that group as well. Several pleaded with him to tell their families.

Ronan glanced up at the sky. It was darkening, which meant that they would most certainly hit if the ship didn't change course. Ronan nodded and ran for the family cabins. He knocked on the first door and a woman answered holding a newborn baby in her arms.

"Be prepared to run for the boats. Don't take anything you can't carry."

The woman tried to ask a question but Ronan was already off to the next cabin. His breath came in gasps now. He was a big man, not used to so many stairs.

The calm of the ship was now gone as everyone asked what was going on and what was being done. Ronan squeezed past them and climbed over the hole so he could climb back into his cell.

He closed his eyes, trying to calm his pounding heart. Even if he'd wanted to escape then, he would have been unable to get far. Several inmates asked him questions, but Declan shushed them and sent them away so Ronan could rest. It may not have changed the captain's mind, but he hoped it would at least get them to safety after the crash.

Screams pulled Ronan from his sleep. He bolted upright to find his inmates yelling. He rubbed his eyes and stood, pushing his way through them so he could talk to the guard.

"What's going on?"

The man's hands shook as he unlocked the cell. "We're about to hit rough waters. You are to go above and wait your turn to board the rescue boats. If any women or children have been missed, make sure they go first."

Ronan thought back to the woman with the newborn. Had she managed to escape? He waited his turn to get out, then move the opposite way. He had to find out if she was okay.

The stairs were still busy, but he was able to get past the others and get to the family deck. He knocked on her door, then opened it. He breathed a sigh of relief when he saw that it was empty. But farther down the hall, they weren't so lucky. A family of three struggled with their young child. Ronan scooped him up and took the mother's hand to help them up to the top deck.

Tears streaked her face as Ronan let go of her hand and set her son in the boat. She climbed in herself and turned to him. "Thank you."

He nodded and ran back in. Three more mothers had to be helped, each with adoration in their eyes as they thanked him. His Selkie charms were at work, even though he hadn't tried to woo them.

It was time to go. Ronan stared out at the ocean and paled when he saw the land just ahead. The ship suddenly leaned to the side, but it wasn't enough. Ronan turned to see what the captain was doing, but it hadn't been him. The first chief stood at the wheel cranking it to the side as far as he could.

Ronan ran for the stairs. He had to get his skin now or it would be lost. The ship leaned ominously, almost knocking Ronan off the staircase. He held tight and slid down the middle pole until he got to the hold.

Several inches of water had come in through a crack. Most of the goods would be ruined. Ronan pushed his way through the cargo, having to stop as the ship leaned the other way. A crate came straight for his torso, but he was able to stop it just in time.

The crates that contained the furs were almost completely submerged. Ronan yanked the lids off until he could sense his skin. He threw furs over his shoulder until his hand finally touched it. He could have cried.

The ship groaned again. Ronan had to get out of there. He climbed up on one of the crates and jumped from one to the next until he could get to the stairs. He held tight to his skin until he was up on the main deck.

"You there. What do you have?" A guard came toward him, baton raised.

Ronan cursed and ran the other way, but another guard stood there. It was now or never. Ronan slipped into his seal skin and dove over the side of the ship. He was free. It was time to go home.

Chapter Seven

Keela

Keela rearranged the fabrics for the hundredth
time that week. Leana had been working on
wearing Maurice down, and while he was pale
and moved slower, he still held tight to Keela's seal skin.

If only Leana hadn't made a pact with Conall not to
end anymore lives. Keela huffed and started on another
pile. Three months she'd been here and her patience was
wearing thin.

"Keela, where are you, lass?" Maurice's voice came
from the front of the store.

Same place she'd been every time he asked. Keela
sighed and went to find him. "Yes, sir?"

Maurice handed her a small box. "We have known
each other for months now. It is time we made it
official."

"Made what official?" Keela opened the box and slammed it shut again. A ring. "No."

"You can't say no to me." His face turned a mottled red. "I own you."

Keela backed up and ran for the back door. A guard stood there with his arms folded. "Save me. Please. He has me trapped in here."

The guard smirked. "He said you'd say that."

"It's the truth." She shrieked as Maurice grabbed onto her arm. "Let me go."

"I think not." Maurice snapped his fingers and the guard lifted Keela and threw her over his shoulder.

Keela screamed until Maurice shoved a cloth into her mouth. She could say nothing as the guard carried her down the street. A few villagers tried to ask questions, but they were quieted. By the time they made it to the small church, Keela was lightheaded from the blood rushing to her head.

They kept the gag in her mouth until the priest was brought in. Keela's jaw ached and tears ran down her face, but she was calm. Leana and Conall were off on a hunt and couldn't help her now. They would be too late. Ronan was long gone. It was up to Keela to save herself.

Maurice grabbed her around the waist and tried to pull her in for a kiss, but she pushed him away. He slapped her and held onto her hands. "You will marry me. You know it is your place to marry your captor, as so many Selkies before you."

Keela froze. He was right. It had happened to her cousin. She smiled. "You're right. But first, may I sing to you?"

Maurice's eyes flashed. "That's better. But not yet. You can sing tonight.

After we are wed."

"Very well." Keela closed her eyes, praying for forgiveness. Ronan would understand.

The priest began, using slightly different words from the ones he'd used for Keela's and Ronan's union. She wondered if that was normal, but then she caught the glint in the priest's eye.

As soon as the wedding ended, Maurice snapped his fingers and the guard threw Keela over his shoulder again. Triona met her at the shop, wringing her hands.

"Let her go. She has done no wrong."

"Wrong? Of course not. My wife did exactly what was asked of her." Maurice grabbed Keela's wrist.

The last thing she saw before the door slammed shut was Triona's look of shock on her face. Keela kept racks of clothes between herself and Maurice's advances. His leer told her it was time to act.

She stopped, and began singing. It surprised Maurice at first, but in his weakened state, he succumbed to her music quickly. His eyes drooped and he fell heavily onto the floor. Keela snatched a handkerchief off one of the racks and danced over to Maurice, singing softer now.

As she moved around him, tightening the scarf, the man didn't move. He was too far gone to even remember to take another breath.

It was here. It had to be. Maurice had held it captive in his shop so that Keela would remember her place. She'd torn the shop apart trying to find her skin with no luck. What has he done with it?

Keela closed her eyes and listened. Felt for it. There. He'd thought he'd been clever, but she could sense the skin above her.

His apartment above the shop was always locked, but Keela found the keys in his pocket. She stepped over him and went to the door. Her hands shook so much that it took several tries to find the right key for the lock.

The room was musty and smelled of decay from the unwashed dishes in his sink. Clearly, he didn't care as much about cleanliness here as he had for the shop. She closed her eyes again, using her other senses to track the skin. When she got to the small room, her mouth turned down in disgust. He had mounted it on the wall, almost as if it was a prize catch. She pulled it down, hugging it tightly to her.

She took the lantern from the back of the shop and dropped it in the middle of floor, igniting the clothes around it. The man had been a plague since she'd met him, and he was finally gone. She stepped out into the cobbled street and walked into the inn, and hugged Triona before leaving again.

"Wait!" Triona gasped as she ran toward Keela. "You can't just leave—" her eyes widened. "What happened there?"

The shop was now fully engulfed in flames. Keela shrugged. "I don't know. Goodbye, Triona. I'll be back as soon as I can find Ronan. If for some reason he comes back before I find him, make him stay here."

Triona nodded. "I will."

Keela walked away from the village but stayed near the coast. She couldn't afford to have her father capture her. She felt for the money in her purse from Bran. Perhaps she could get a horse at the next village.

When her energy lagged, Keela would walk along the beach with her feet in the water. She was careful to never allow the skin to touch the water. That would have called to her father immediately.

As evening neared, Keela knew she couldn't keep going. It was time for her to become a seal again. She slipped it on, sighing at the comfort it brought. She was herself again. Maurice had done some damage to the skin, but it would heal once it was back in the ocean.

She dove into the water, kicking as hard she could get into deeper water. The water was smooth on her skin, and she wondered how she'd ever survived without it.

She instinctively headed for her kingdom and had gone a few leagues before realizing her mistake.

Ronan was out there somewhere and she had to find him.

Chapter Eight

Ronan

onan broke through the surface of the waves and climbed up onto the small island. He'd been swimming for two days and it felt as though he hadn't moved. He could feel Ireland calling to him like a beacon. He knew the direction he had to go, but with every league he crossed, he felt that the ocean grew another five leagues wide.

Soon he would be entering sea monster territory, and he wasn't looking forward to fighting him off. He'd already caught sight of a few of them, but thankfully they were in the distance. He was not small compared to other Selkies, but the other creatures would treat him like a play toy if he were to go up against them.

A horn blared in the distance. Ronan turned and grinned. A ship. Just like he'd hoped. He stripped his seal skin and used its magic to shrink it. No need for questions. He grabbed branches from the trees and started a fire with leftover magic that had begun fading as soon as he pulled off the seal skin. He kept the fire going with as much smoke as possible to flag down the ship.

The thought that this could be people from his past ship crossed his mind, but at this point he needed to get back to his Keela.

The ship slowed as it came closer and a man waved his arm from the ship. Ronan waved back and went straight for the life preserver that they threw overboard. It was hard to take his skin with him, but he wasn't about to let it go. As long as he held onto it, he could use the magic it held to shield it, but it sapped his energy. The sooner he could get up onto the ship and dry off, the better.

The captain stood on the deck waiting for Ronan. He held out a hand. "Welcome. Have you been exiled here long?"

"Aye, my ship wrecked a few days ago, and I haven't been able to find a way home." It was mostly the truth. He just didn't have to mention where the wreck had happened.

"Of course, of course. We are headed for England with urgent news about a tragic accident near Australia. We won't be able to stop on the way, so if you need to be dropped off before, we'll have to send you off with a life raft on the way."

"England is just fine. I can find my way to Ireland from there." Ronan threw in more of an Irish lilt than he normally had.

The man's eyebrows rose. "You're quite away from home. What brought you all this way?"

"I'd hoped to find a new life for myself. Turns out, I made the biggest mistake of my life and now I'm heading back to make up for it. I plan to marry my girl."

"Ah, she roped you in, did she? Well, you'll see her again soon enough. My first mate will help you find a cabin. For now, I must get this ship back up to full speed." He tipped his hat and left, while another man stepped forward.

"Let's get you warmed up. My wife is off looking for extra clothing for you and will meet us in your cabin. It's a bit small, but it will do."

Ronan smiled. Anything would be better than the conditions he'd lived in over the last few months. "Thank you. I'm sure it's just fine."

The cabin was about the size of the room that he'd had at the inn. It was just large enough for a bed and a table, but he would be alone.

"If there is anything else we can do for you, don't hesitate to ask." The first mate paused. "If you don't mind me asking, where did your boat sink? We wanted to make sure that we don't run into any debris."

Ronan should have known they'd ask something like that. "It was farther out to sea. You passed it already."

"Ah. Very good. Oh, here's your change of clothes now." He moved over so the captain's wife could enter.

She was a short, round woman who had smile lines around her eyes. "Here you go, dearie. Get warmed up. We serve dinner in an hour."

Ronan bowed slightly and took the items from her. "Thank you."

As soon as they left, Ronan changed and dropped onto the bed. While the mattress was still thin, it was molded to him. It wasn't until he relaxed that he realized just how tired he was. Even as a seal, traveling all that way had been taxing. He rolled over and pictured Keela as he drifted off. *I'm coming, love.*

It was official. Ronan was bored out of his mind. While the prison ship had been less than satisfactory, he at least had people to talk to—or to ignore. Everyone on this ship was nice enough, but he spent most of his days alone. The passengers were from high society, so he had no idea how to interact with them.

The ocean was beginning to change, and the longing had grown stronger. Ireland was growing closer every day and he was ready to be home already. Had Keela waited for him? He had to believe that she did. Even though the women on this ship seemed to go out of their way to draw his attention, he only had eyes for Keela.

As the ship approached the waters of his homeland, Ronan couldn't take it anymore. He waited until all but the captain had gone to bed, then crept out onto the deck. He pulled his seal skin on and shook himself to make sure it fit right. He checked to make sure no one was watching, then dove into the water. It was a long way down, but with his seal skin, he cut through the water easily.

He stayed underwater and dove deeper. He'd heard enough about sonar over the time he'd been on the ship that he knew he had to get away from the ship as soon as possible.

The water had a chill to it that he'd missed terribly. He sang his song of longing, hoping that Keela would hear before anyone else. He wasn't sure where he'd find her, but the plan was to head back to the village where he'd found her.

Sounds came from ahead, making Ronan slow. There was a group of Selkies ahead. It was too far out to sea for it to be Keela's people. This could be good or bad. He was careful with his signals now, but he continued to call for her. A group waited for him as he grew closer to land.

"State your business." The largest of the Selkies glared at him.

"I am simply here to find my wife. Keela. Have you seen or heard from her?"

The Selkies exchanged glances before the leader shook his head. "There have been no other Selkies here for years. Where are you returning from?"

Ronan sighed. There was no reason to keep the story from them, so he told them everything had happened. "May I go now? I must find her."

"You may pass, but we must warn you. The king is furious that his daughter left him. If you were to find her, I advise you to stay as far away as you can."

"I intend to do exactly that. Thank you." Ronan continued on his journey. Other creatures became more prominent and soon he saw other Selkies he knew. Some greeted him while others swam the other way.

Word had obviously gotten out about him. But hopefully that would mean that they would know where Keela was. Someone had to know where to find her.

Chapter Nine

Keela

Keela promised herself that she could rest if she could just make it one more league. But what was the point when every league looked exactly the same as the last one? Every moment she wondered if she should turn back. But she knew she needed to find Ronan.

She glanced up to see the placement of the sun and she was surprised to find that it had almost set. She allowed herself to stop swimming and sink to the ground below. She would sleep for an hour or so and then continue on.

The sea creatures scattered as she fell and provided a blanket of seaweed for her to be more comfortable.

A net came over Keela, trapping her. She struggled to break free, but it was no use. Her father's guards held her tight as they made their way back to the kingdom.

"Please release me." Keela relaxed against the bonds. The fatigue from swimming for too long had sapped all of her strength.

"You know we can't do that." One of the older Selkies looked down at her, sadness in his eyes. "You should not have tried to leave the island."

Keela glared at him. "You know why I had to do it. You were the one who suggested that I follow my heart."

"Not if it meant going after Ronan," he snapped.

"So, you would tell me to stay miserable for the rest of my life."

The older Selkie stayed silent for a moment. "Yes."

Keela sighed. She knew the man didn't mean that. Father demanded complete obedience from his guards, and that included carrying out his orders. She would have a talk with him when she was delivered to him.

She was surprised when the guards took her straight to the palace. Normally Father loved to keep his prisoners waiting for an audience for days or even months before finally gaining an audience with him. And she most certainly didn't expect to have any leniency from him.

The guards dropped the net on the floor of the throne room. Keela stood and shook the net off, then held her head high. He would not see her as weak.

Father sat in his throne, staring down at Keela. Their last meeting in this room ran through her head. He'd been so angry that she had gone behind his back to meet with Ronan. She had barely been able to defend herself before he'd exiled her to live on land. It had been meant as a punishment of the worst kind, but it had turned into a blessing instead.

"Hello, daughter. I'm glad to see that you've been reunited with your seal skin."

"Don't pretend that you care."

Father grumbled. "Don't speak to me that way."

She stood up straighter. He didn't intimidate her. Not anymore. "Why did you send for me?"

"To prevent you from making a serious mistake. If you were to leave my protected waters, I would no longer be able to ensure your safety. I couldn't have that happen."

"But you could make me marry a human? That is so much worse, Father." Keela glared at him. "You doomed my husband by putting him on that ship. He was one of your people too. By keeping me prisoner, you've made sure that he'll never return here. If your humble servants knew that was how you treated those who you rule, there would be an uprising."

Father snorted. "He was hardly one of my people. His family could barely pay their taxes, and they hadn't been to court to pay their respects in years."

Keela's mouth dropped open. "His family was poor because of the taxes you placed on them. There are many others in the same boat. I told you once before to watch out for those people. Are you really going to defend your actions?"

"Guards, take her away. Put her in prison until I can decide what to do with her. Sending her off to live as a human was clearly not the answer. I must find another way to punish her." He stared in disgust as the guards dragged her off.

Keela kept his gaze until they went around the corner. She would not give him the satisfaction of seeing her cry. He hadn't earned her respect, and he most certainly wasn't going to have the satisfaction of watching her go kicking and screaming. She would be back in his presence again soon enough and he would see what keeping his people living in fear for so long would get him.

Chapter Ten

Ronan

Ronan passed a group of old friends and doubled back. "Have you seen Keela?"

They shook their heads, but he knew they were lying by the way they avoid his gaze. He sighed. She'd been through here, and worse, they'd been threatened by their king. At least he knew where to find her.

Ronan headed straight for the palace and instead of going straight to the throne room, he went to find Keela's mother.

She sat in her room with her ladies-in-waiting. Her eyes widened when she saw Ronan. "What are you doing here?"

"Saving your daughter. Have you seen her?" Ronan knew she wouldn't have. She was treated almost as badly as the rest of the kingdom.

"She was sent off." She gasped. "But then so were you. Are you saying she's back?" The hope in her voice broke Ronan's heart.

He put a hand over hers. "She's here and I worry that she's been thrown in the dungeon. Please. You need to help me get her out of there."

Her mother nodded. "It's going to take a little time to get it set up, but I have to make sure that she's free, and that the king can never do this again. I won't have him doing this to my daughter."

"Perfect. Where do we start?"

"Spread the word of what has happened, but you cannot let on that you're here. Keep a low profile. He cannot know you're back. I'll work on it from my side."

Ronan nodded. "Of course, Highness."

"Go. Meet me here first thing in the morning with as many people as you can find."

Ronan bowed and left her room. What they were about to do was extremely dangerous. If the king suspected any sort of revolt, those who went up against him would be dead before they had a chance to fight.

He started with the people in the outskirts of the city. "The king has the princess as a captive. We can't allow this to happen. She treated you well, brought you food and the money you needed to pay her father's taxes. Are you willing to let that happen?"

Murmurs ran through the people as they spread the

news. Ronan then moved onto the next group of people and continued through the city until he'd made it up to the guards. They'd hear it soon enough, and he couldn't let them know where he was.

The prison was heavily guarded, as it would have to be to keep people from rescuing the princess. Ronan moved quickly, knocking out the guards as quickly as possible so they couldn't alert the others. He took the keys from one of the guards and released the prisoners, explaining what was going on as he went.

By the time he reached Keela's door, he had a large following of people to back him up. He opened the door and found his beloved Keela lying on the floor. She sat up and let out a sob.

"You're here." She stood and threw her arms around him. "I'd begun to believe I would never see you again."

"An ocean wasn't about keep me away from you." Ronan led her out of the prison. "Are you ready to overthrow your father as leader?"

Keela hesitated before nodding. "How will we do that? He'll try to stop us."

Ronan waited until they walked around the corner to answer. "Oh, it won't just be the two of us."

The crowd was even larger than when Ronan had left them to let her out of her cell. Selkies as far as he could see.

"They'll help us."

Keela smiled. "Shall we go say hello to my father?"

"After you, my love."

They left the prison and moved toward the throne room, followed by thousands of Selkies. Keela's mother stood outside the room with her own guards. She rushed to Keela and pulled her into a hug.

"Oh, my darling. I thought you were gone forever."

"So did I." Keela looked up at the guards. "Are you sure we can trust them?"

Her mother laughed. "I picked my own guards long ago. Come. Let's stop your father."

Ronan opened the doors and allowed the queen through first. He and Keela waited just outside and waited for the cue.

"Hello, Highness. Fine morning, isn't it?"

"What are you doing here? I thought you were off hunting with your ladies-in-waiting." The king's voice was angry, and Ronan had to hold Keela back from running in to defend her mother. They had to wait.

The queen didn't speak until she stood just in front of him. "I'd planned to today. Until I discovered something rather upsetting."

"Oh? And what's that, dear?"

"It seems that our daughter is back and you neglected to tell me."

Keela giggled and had to cover her mouth. Ronan shot her a warning look and peeked through the door to see the king's reaction. He was as stunned as Ronan had hoped.

"Your daughter is a traitor to her people," the king spat out.

"No, Highness. I don't believe she is." The queen paused for effect. This was it. Ronan and Keela both took the handle of the throne room doors. "You are."

At the count of three, Ronan and Keela walked into the throne room, hand-in-hand. Keela smiled. "Hello, Daddy."

His eyes widened. "Guards! Why is she free?"

But there was no one there to answer him. The guards had fled as soon as they'd seen the crowd of people. Just as Ronan had hoped they would.

"Oh, Daddy. I warned you about this months ago. Treat your people right, or they would turn on you. Remember?"

The king sputtered. "You cannot speak to your king that way."

The queen laughed. "Oh, but she can. Because as far as I'm concerned, you are no longer king."

"How dare you? You think you can overthrow me?" The king reached for his staff.

"I can't. But they can."

The throne room doors opened again and Selkies spilled into the room. From the poorest Selkie, to the most elite. Ronan's chest swelled with pride for his beautiful Keela. She'd treated her people well, and these people knew it.

"You can step down gracefully, or you can go fighting every step of the way. But, Father, your time as king has come to an end." Keela's eyes were hard as she stared into her father's.

Ronan steeled himself to rush the throne if her father resisted. But that wasn't necessary. The queen yanked the crown from his head and a guard took his staff.

The king seemed so fragile being led away from the throne room. Ronan was almost disappointed that he hadn't put up a fight. He would have loved to have the satisfaction of punching him for the way he'd treated Keela.

A chant began among the people. Keela's name. It grew until everyone—including the queen—chanted her name.

Keela moved up to the front to stand next to her mother. Tears ran down her face as she picked up the crown on the ground. She dusted it off, and placed it on her mother's head. The chant died off as they looked at each other uncertainly. Ronan felt the ache of having to lose her again as she became the next ruler. There would be laws to pass before she would be allowed to be with him.

"If it is the will of the people, I will leave the

kingdom in my mother's name for a little longer. She is good and she will take good care of you. I need time to reunite with my husband. But I will be back."

As one, the crowd dropped to their knees and bowed. Ronan stood in shock as she turned and handed the staff to her mother. "Treat them well, Mother. I'll be back soon."

Her mother kissed her hand and Keela stepped off the stage. She grabbed Ronan's hand and together, they ran out of the throne room. As they left the palace, Ronan stopped and turned to his wife.

"Why?"

"Because I waited too long to be with you. And because Mother deserves her chance to rule this people the correct way. I know they'll be in good hands."

That was enough for Ronan. They turned and fled the city.

Chapter Eleven

Keela

Keela stood in her blue dress and waited for Ronan to open the door to the inn. She entered, and looked around for Triona.

Her dear friend stood at one of the tables taking an order. As soon as she saw Keela, she dropped her paper and ran toward her. "I thought I'd never see you again."

"I had to admit, I thought the same thing." Keela pulled away and took Triona's hands in hers. "We were wondering if we could stay here for a while. I'm not quite ready to rule a kingdom yet."

"Of course. Da, look who's here."

Bran stared at Keela and Ronan for a moment before shouting toward the kitchen. "Start the goose and a lamb. There will be a feast tonight."

A cheer filled the common room. Keela took

Ronan's hand in hers. The palace underwater was where she would rule one day, but for now this was where her heart was.

The feast carried late into the night with people traveling for miles to attend. Leana and Conall sat in one of the booths Keela and Ronan listening to their adventures since they'd left the village.

Leana leaned back and pouted. "I missed all the fun."

"Dearie, we were off fighting the Dearg Due. We were hardly missing any excitement."

"Yes, but she's old news. We already fought her once."

Conall laughed. "Darling, you took down a vampire who has roamed this land for over a millennium. That is not old news."

"Still. I would have liked to see Keela dethrone her father."

Keela laughed. She would miss these people when she left. The sea had already begun to call her home. She knew it wouldn't be much longer before she'd have to answer, but for now she would sit in the booth of a small village inn and enjoy her time with friends.

The door burst open suddenly. A man stood there with terror in his eyes. "It's coming. Famine, disease.

Headed this way. It's already claimed several farms in the area. Run. Gather up what you can."

Leana smiled and turned to Conall. "Ready? I haven't seen a fear gorta in decades."

"I told you we still had fun." Conall leaned forward and kissed her.

"Can we come?" Keela asked.

Ronan glanced between them, but said nothing as the four of them left the inn. Keela took his hand as they strode out of the village. The kingdom and the call of the ocean could wait one more day. She had another adventure to go on.

Acknowledgments

For those who have read my books, it's common knowledge that I love fairy tales. But most especially, I love Celtic fairy tales. It happened on one fateful day when I wrote about a girl with extraordinary luck who had a leprechaun suddenly show up at her doorstep. It was not what I had expected, but I have never once regretted the journey it took me on.

I'm always looking for a new fairy tale to write, and Keela just felt right. The day I watched *Song of the Sea* with my daughter, I knew I needed to write a about Selkie.

When coming up with the storyline for this book, I happened upon the story of a ship that had set out from Ireland with two hundred and fifty prisoners, along with their crew. Babette Smith wrote a book called *The Luck of the Irish: How a Shipload of Convicts Survived the Wreck of the Hive to Make a New Life in Australia* that talked about what had happened on this ship, and I was hooked. I'd gone back and forth trying to decide if it was right for this story, but when the time came, I knew it was perfect.

I want to thank my mom for reading the book and keeping me going. Also, my cousin, Molly, who asked for a copy before it was ever written. I told her to keep on bugging me about it, and I'm glad she did. Thank you to my beta readers—Chrystal Meyer, Alena Johnson, Katie Armstrong, Janelle Fuhriman, Robin Bench, Erin James, Stephanie Wright, Sarah Gardiner, George McVey, and Angelique Conger. You're my lifesavers!

Thank you to my family for always being an amazing support, and to you my readers, for loving my stories.

ABOUT THE AUTHOR

Jaclyn is an Idaho farm girl who grew up loving to read. She developed a love for writing as a senior in high school, when her dad jokingly said she was the next Dr. Seuss (not even close, but very sweet). She met her husband, Steve, at BYU, and they have six happy, crazy children who encourage her to keep writing. After owning a bookstore and running away to have adventures in Australia, they settled back down in their home in Utah. Jaclyn now spends her days herding her kids to various activities and trying to remember what she was supposed to do next. Her books include; Endless: A Modern Cinderella Tale, Timeless: A Sleeping Beauty Tale, Fearless: A Modern Rapunzel Tale; Magicians of the Deep; the Luck series--Stolen Luck, Twist of Luck, Best of Luck, More Than Just Luck, No Such Luck, and Just My Luck, a novella.

More books by Jaclyn Weist

<u>Lost in a Fairy Tale</u>

Timeless: A Sleeping Beauty Tale
Fearless: A Rapunzel Tale
Endless: A Modern Cinderella Tale

<u>The Luck Series</u>

Stolen Luck
Twist of Luck
Best of Luck
More Than Just Luck
No Such Luck
Just My Luck, a novella

<u>The Gates of Atlantis</u>

Magicians of the Deep

<u>Celtic Fairy Tale Romances</u>
Leana
Keela

If you enjoyed this book,

please leave a review at:

Amazon.com

Goodreads.com

For signed copies, or to

contact Jaclyn, visit:

www.jaclynweist.com

CPSIA information can be obtained
at www.ICGtesting.com
Printed in the USA
BVHW041922271120
594367BV00034B/623

9 781981 861507